SPIDER'S WEB

Allie Jordan

A KISMET™ Romance

METEOR PUBLISHING CORPORATION
Bensalem, Pennsylvania

KISMET™ is a trademark of Meteor Publishing Corporation

Copyright © 1991 Sandra Chastain
Cover Art Copyright © 1991 Sterling Brown

All rights reserved.

No part of this book may be reproduced, stored in a retrieval system, or transmitted in any form, by any means, including mechanical, electronic, photocopying, recording or otherwise, without prior written permission of the publisher, Meteor Publishing Corporation, 3369 Progress Drive, Bensalem, PA 19020.

First Printing May 1991.

ISBN: 1-878702-40-8

All the characters in this book are fictitious. Any resemblance to actual persons, living or dead, is purely coincidental.

Printed in the United States of America

For all the grandmothers everywhere who still believe in romance and the magic of love.

ALLIE JORDAN

Allie Jordan is as Southern as moonlight and magnolias. After thirty-five years of marriage and eighteen romance novels, she still believes in the fantasy of romance. When Allie isn't writing, she's enjoying her three grandchildren, visiting antique flea markets with her husband or teaching creative writing.

ONE

"Gran! Gran! Bug!"

The towheaded little boy ran into the house, screaming at the top of his lungs.

"Now, Charlie, a little bug is nothing to be afraid of." Silvia Fitzpatrick patted her grandson's head reassuringly and began to put away the groceries.

Silvia couldn't remember her daughter Hallie being afraid of anything as a child. She wouldn't have forgotten that. What she had mercifully forgotten were the hazards of a shopping trip with a two-year-old until she'd reached the check-out counter with a strange box of cefeal and a large red spoon in her cart.

"No, Gran." The little boy buried his head persistently against Silvia's legs in terror. "Big bug. Big!"

"Hello in the kitchen?" There was a bold knock

on the kitchen door, overridden by an even bolder masculine voice. "Hallie? Are you in there?"

Hallie? What now? At thirty-six, Associate Professor Silvia Fitzpatrick thought that her life was in order. As a member of the staff of the English department of the University of Georgia, she was exactly where she wanted to be. There might still be a few people around who remembered her as the brash teenager who charged around town in her grandfather's old red pickup truck but she'd lived down most of her mistakes in judgment.

Now Hallie had moved back home with her young son, Charlie, becoming a second generation single parent. Suddenly history was repeating itself, except that Hallie's decision was by choice. Or was it? All Silvia's old guilt came sweeping back and she didn't know how to stop it.

Silvia shook off her thoughts. "Don't be afraid, darling," Silvia whispered to Charlie, and called out, "Hallie isn't here. I'm not sure when she'll be back."

Opening a package of Oreo cookies, Silvia handed one to the two-year-old, a bribe she would never have offered to his mother. "Why don't you go and play with your toys, Charlie? The bug is probably long gone," she said comfortingly as she took the ice cream from the disposable plastic grocery bag.

"No," the child insisted, taking the cookie, but making no effort to devour it as he usually did. "Gran, swat bug?"

Silvia could see that Charlie was really scared. "OK. You go and play and I'll get rid of the bug." She lifted the fly swatter from its magnetic hook on the refrigerator and held it up as proof of her battle plan.

Satisfied, Charlie turned and ran off as fast as his chubby legs would go.

There was a second knock, a more forceful second knock, that turned into a pounding that vibrated the house. That person was still at her back screen door. He seemed very determined. Silvia didn't know why that should surprise her. Hallie was the same way. Like mother like daughter—determined.

Turning, Silvia stepped out onto the porch, still holding the raised fly swatter in one hand and the ice cream she was about to put away in the other.

"Help! Please let me in before one of your neighbors calls the law. I'm afraid that I'm in rather an embarrassing position out here."

Silvia shook her head in disbelief. She closed her eyes and opened them again. She had to be hallucinating. No, a little secret lust now and then, but Silvia Fitzpatrick never hallucinated. Standing on her porch was a six-foot-tall, barefoot man, wearing a pair of disgustingly tight, red running shorts and black diamond-patterned dragon wings which seemed to be attached to a feathery Mardi Gras-style mask covering most of his face.

The thought that she should have brought a shotgun instead of a fly swatter flitted through her mind. "Who are you?" Silvia whispered, cleared her throat, and added, "And why are you knocking on my door?"

"I'm Fletcher Sims and I'm hiding."

"Why?"

"I'm not exactly dressed, and there is a woman standing in the upstairs window next door with exterminator eyes."

"That's Honey, and I'd say that exterminating is the right idea."

"Please don't swat me. Just get Mrs. Fitzpatrick for me."

"*I'm* Mrs. Fitzpatrick, and for the life of me I can't recall that I was expecting an insect."

"You're Silvia?"

"No, to you, I'm Mrs. Fitzpatrick."

"I'm sorry, but, well, you certainly aren't what I expected."

"Oh, and what did you expect, Mr. Sims, a ladybug?"

"I expected Hallie's mother to be . . . well, *motherly*, not . . . well, let's just say you're no June Cleaver."

"No, I'm not June Cleaver, but even if I were, I wouldn't be as out of place as . . . the Molting Fly. What do you want . . . Mr. . . . what did you say your name is?"

"My friends and most of my enemies call me Fletch. I don't know which category you fall into yet, but couldn't we discuss this inside? Hallie told me you'd be happy about this."

Hallie? Happy about what? What had her daughter done now? Hallie's sudden elopement with one of the college football players when she was still a high school senior had taken Silvia by surprise. Stoically, she had taken the blame for her daughter's action. She'd set a poor example. After all, she'd eloped when she was a senior, too. Publicly she'd been a loving and supportive mother to Hallie, working even harder to earn the respect she so desperately needed.

Now the man standing on the other side of her screen door was a new challenge to her self-imposed control and a threat that she wasn't able to define. Silvia unlatched the door and stepped back, allowing Fletcher Sims to step inside the screened porch.

"All right. Since you seem to know Hallie, Mr. Sims, I suppose you can come in. Is this some kind of fraternity thing? No, you're too old for that. Never mind the explanation, I'm not sure that I even want to know. Just tell me what you want from Hallie."

"Her help, but I'll take yours instead."

"If you expect either of us to help you, you'd better put some clothes on first."

"I would, but I'm locked out."

"Of where?"

"Your garage."

"A winged creature is moving into my garage? I suppose you're going to tell me that you're building a nest."

"In so many words. I guess you don't know yet. I'm your new tenant."

Fletcher Sims groaned silently. He'd known this was a mistake when Greg Evans and his impulsive student had suggested the garage apartment. In fact, the idea of living on a college campus had been a bad idea from the start.

"My tenant? Since when?" There was no way Silvia could keep the surprise out of her voice.

Fletcher watched his new landlady with growing dismay. According to Greg, Hallie's mother was a devoted teacher and a good friend. She also ran some kind of public relations business in her home. None of these attributes suggested that she would look fantastic.

Granted, she was wearing tailored gray slacks and a soft shiny blouse with pearl buttons and matching pearl earrings. Her dark hair was straight, swinging about her face with a jaunty bounce. There was nothing particularly striking about her. Yet, there was a sleek elegance about her that he hadn't expected, a suggestion of fire that wasn't quite concealed by her calm demeanor.

Silvia Fitzpatrick had asked him a question. Considering the raised fly swatter she was holding, he decided he'd better answer.

"I'm sorry, Mrs. Fitzpatrick, I thought your daughter called you."

"She didn't. How did you get here?"

"You weren't at home when I drove up. I parked on the street so that I wouldn't block your drive. I was going to bring the last load in and then come back to introduce myself. In the meantime, I seem to have gotten myself locked out. Do you have an extra key?"

Partially covered by the blue-green iridescent feathers of his mask, the man's Mediterranean blue eyes scrutinized her intently. There was a definite hint of amusement lurking beneath their cool surface. Silvia didn't know what Greg had been thinking of when he and Hallie came up with the idea of her garage as living quarters for the man standing in the kitchen doorway.

For one absurd moment she decided that Fletcher Sims belonged at the top of a Mayan pyramid. She'd seen pictures of men like him in history books and movies but never in real life. His midnight-black hair was slightly long, curling beneath the feathery winged headdress. Sleek, tanned, and barefoot, his body looked wild and sensual. El Condor had traveled through a time warp and landed on her back porch.

Then he smiled.

Even while his lips were crooking sensually she saw something in his eyes that said he wasn't totally self-confident about his presence here.

Charlie was right. Now, before it was too late, while she still had her senses about her, she ought to swat the big bug. But those compelling eyes, and a smile that seemed to reach out and wrap its warmth around her immobilized her usual control. For a moment she had a crazy flashback from the past, a remembering of the power of desire and the agony of facing its results.

Short of an erotic dream, Silvia couldn't remember a more incredible exchange. What she should do was step back into the kitchen and call the campus police. She was a member of the college faculty, she deserved protection. Instead she was standing here swapping wisecracks with a winged predator.

"An extra key," he prompted as if he could

read her mind and knew she'd lost his question. "Please?"

"I don't know. It's been so long since anybody lived out there that I didn't even know that the lock worked."

"It works," he said in a deep, rich voice. "I can attest to that. I dropped a load of books. Just as I turned around to pick them up the wind blew the door shut on my stinger and broke that sucker off. Now I'm locked out."

She was caught up in his determination to continue the wiseguy routine. "Broke your stinger? Oh, dear. That must be a real blow to a big bug like you. Why not just grow another? An insect without a stinger could be in big trouble in a little college town like this. What will folks say?"

Not only was she inexplicably unable to evict the man, but she also was matching him quip for quip, the kind of clever repartee that she never indulged in. Her words seemed to reassure him, as though they'd both learned their lines and were following the script. Silvia didn't smile, but she felt an odd kind of exhilaration sweep over her.

"Snappy reply, darling. That's an even better comeback than the line I was going to use. I like a woman with wit and a quick mind."

Wit and a quick mind? What was wrong with her? Nobody had ever in her life credited her with having a quick wit. There'd been a time when she'd been voted The Girl We'd Most Like To Spend The Weekend With On Top Of Stone Mountain. That had been because she'd always had fun, not because she was funny. And that was a long time ago.

The ozone layer, perhaps some voodoo spell had loosened her tongue and sharpened her mental edge. Silvia Fitzpatrick would never carry on such a conversation with a stranger, even if he did look like a Mayan god. She would never allow herself to reveal her inner feelings. This had to be an out-of-body experience. She was still in the kitchen with Charlie. She closed her eyes and shook her head.

No, the bug man was still there. She'd better do something—quick.

"All right, Mr. Sims. Let's see if we can get this misunderstanding settled. I have things to do this morning."

"Ah, Silvia darling, just when it was getting interesting. I like a woman who knows her own mind, especially when she's a real lady. I was about to ask you to fly away with me."

That did it. Silvia took a deep breath to calm her rapid heartbeat. She was a disciplined person. She never lost her temper. But one look at Fletcher Sims's wicked smile and the words just blurted out.

"You listen to me, you winged . . . crow! Don't call me darling." Oh, goodness, she was doing it again. She squared her shoulders and firmly lowered her voice. "What I want you to do is take your bad lines and your bare buns and be gone before I lower the boom. I have no intention of renting my garage to anybody."

"Why not?"

"The stove doesn't work and I'm not sure about the shower. And stop trying to metragrobolize my mind by calling me a lady as though I were some kind of museum piece. I'm sorry. There has been a mistake."

"Metragrobolize? Fool around with your mind? Never! Don't apologize, Silvia. Women are two for a dollar, but a lady who plays with words? Definitely my kind of challenge. I knew this Nightwing costume would come in handy."

"What's a night wing? Never mind, I'm not sure that I want to know."

She couldn't see the shape of his face clearly. Veiled by the mask its definition seemed to change depending on the angle of his glance. But his eyes were definitely wicked. He had a meet-me-after-dark smile and an easy air of confidence that gave reality to the absurd and made their conversation feel wonderfully normal.

"The Nightwing is an island spirit bird that comes in the darkest part of the moon to plant beautiful words in the mind. The natives of Hario Splendor could tell you about it. They gave me this costume as a parting gift when I left."

"And you flew into Athens, Georgia, did you? I don't know what you're talking about. I don't want to know what you're talking about. We've already had the witch trials in this country and that was three hundred years ago. Please, Mr. Sims, my daughter is known to act on the spur of the moment. While she means well, her decisions aren't always wise."

"And you don't, do you?"

"Do what?"

"Act on the spur of the moment?"

"Never. I always consider all the options."

"Sounds dull to me."

"Not dull, prudent."

"Dull, prudent, same thing. Such a waste. But not to worry, darling. I'm just the one to teach you how to let go."

"Really, Mr. Sims, please! How did you get here wearing that outfit? Tell me that the world didn't see you."

"I'm an ordinary traveler. Your friend and mine, Greg Evans, head of the English department, loaned me his Jeep. That's where I ran into your daughter, at Greg's."

"At Greg's apartment?" Silvia couldn't keep the surprise from her voice. She knew that Hallie's lifestyle was vastly different from hers. But she'd worked with Greg for almost ten years and she'd never been to his apartment.

"No, at his office. I drove him to work and borrowed his Jeep to look for an apartment. By the first of September, there are no vacant apartments in a college town. Greg thought I'd set a poor example for the student body by camping out on the football field. He remembered your garage and convinced Hallie you wouldn't mind renting it to me—unless you have a better idea."

"Oh, I have a better idea all right. Just find yourself a very large tree!"

"Ah, Silvia. I wish I could live in a nest, but I can't. Except for Greg's Jeep, I'm totally earthbound."

"If this is the way you normally dress, I don't know why Greg should worry about where you live."

"Oh, my Nightwing costume. I should never have unpacked it last night, but Greg wanted to see it. After I got it out I just laid it on top of my duffel bag. Wearing it seemed to be the best way of transporting it from the Jeep to the apartment."

Silvia closed her eyes and shook her head. She'd never had an encounter with anyone like this man before. Maintaining control of a situation was a trait she'd mastered years ago. She could handle this . . . this insect. She simply had to approach him logically.

"Mr. Sims, Hallie didn't know the condition of the apartment or she wouldn't have rented it to you. I'm sorry if you've been inconvenienced, but I'm afraid that you'll have to find other accommodations."

"How? Everything is rented."

"But . . ." He was right. She knew it. There weren't enough dorms, and the students took up every available room for thirty miles. "All right," she agreed reluctantly, "you can stay for a few days, but only until you can find something else."

Fletcher Sims peeled the mask from his head and put a serious expression on his face. He was losing the woman and that was a new experience for him. Not only was losing bad for his image, but he decided that she intrigued him in a way that he didn't quite understand. As usual, he was behaving like Spider Malone, the devil-may-care hero of the men's adventure novels he wrote. That wouldn't work here. He was coming on too strong, too soon.

"It's hard to believe that you're Hallie's mother," he said sincerely. "You don't look old enough to have a daughter. I was expecting some matronly widow woman, not," Fletcher added under his breath, allowing Spider's personality to slip out, "not a beautiful woman who doesn't look old enough to have a married daughter."

Fletcher groaned to himself, allowing the costume's wings to slide off his shoulders and hang down beside his body. Silvia Fitzpatrick was exactly the kind of woman he should dislike. Greg Evans had said that, to everyone's dismay, Silvia was determined to cast herself in the role of college professor, businesswoman, and pious widow. But Fletcher sensed a mass of honest emotions hidden beneath the surface. Why then was he finding ways to make her eyes sizzle with anger? *Stop it*, he told himself, *you're not here to respond to a woman with flashing eyes and lips demanding to be kissed.*

Silvia blinked hard. He should have left the mask on. She didn't want to be any more aware of his strong face, his hair as black as a raven's wing, his sleepy eyes giving off a lush sensual message that he made no attempt to control. But she was being held by graceful dark brows raised in question above sapphire-blue eyes and long thick lashes.

"I not only have a daughter, Mr. Sims," Silvia said hoarsely, "I'm a grandmother."

What she was certain was that his normal repartee evaporated in the intensity of the moment. He was staring at her in silence, just as confused as she. Finally, just as she thought she might scream, he spoke.

"A grandmother, a very young grandmother. Yes. That's all right, you know. In Hario Splendor, women marry by the time they're twelve and often have grandchildren by the time they're twenty-five. They say the experience of life keeps them forever young."

He was doing it again, hypnotizing her into submission with words. At the same time his eyes were undressing her and reclothing her in a heated second that even she couldn't misinterpret.

"Or maybe forever old," Silvia managed with a stern frown, shaking off the power of his presence. "This isn't Hario Splendor, wherever that is, Mr. Sims. This is Athens, Georgia, and if you're interested in my daughter, I have to tell you that you're much too old for Hallie. I don't approve of any of this. I plan to speak to Greg Evans right away."

"Silvia, at this point I barely know Hallie. I simply met her in Greg's office. Please, I've been traveling for a long time and I'm very tired. I'm probably going to regret this, but the truth is, if I had to make a choice, I'd say that it's her mother I'm going to make love to. And at this moment, that thought doesn't make me any happier than it does you. We'll simply have to get through it."

"Yoo hoo! Silvia? Is everything all right?" Honey Watts, resplendent in a purple print caftan, plunged through the hedge separating Silvia's house from the driveway next door.

At the same time, "Gran, bad bug gone?" Charlie came through the door from the den.

The last simultaneous arrival was Hallie, slamming the front door as she dashed down the hall. "Hello, Charlie darling. Mother, did Fletch get here yet?"

To her neighbor Silvia said, "I'm not sure, Honey, but I'd be careful. A large insect seems to have taken up residence in the garage and I don't know what it feeds on."

To her grandson: "Charlie, the bug is a friend of your mommy's. Let her swat it."

To her startled daughter, Silvia handed her the fly swatter, turned, and walked slowly through the kitchen and into her office, closing the door firmly behind.

Becoming a twenty-four year old widow with a seven-year-old daughter had been difficult, but she was certain that she'd been a good mother. All the neighbors had remarked on how level-headed she'd become in the face of disaster. She hadn't been, but she'd forced herself to mirror that image. Never again would she allow herself to give way to emotional tirades. It was the only way she could live with the guilt she felt over her young husband's death. If they hadn't fallen in love, if she hadn't gotten pregnant, if she hadn't decided to have the baby, if they hadn't quarreled, John might not have died.

There'd been an insurance policy, but that hadn't been enough. Silvia took the money and went to college, supplementing their income by typing term papers at home and writing an occasional résumé.

As a college senior she'd helped one of the young advertising students compose a sales brochure, revealing a talent for composition and design that she hadn't known she possessed, and Options, Inc., was officially born.

She'd finally taken out a business license and an ad to announce the opening of the secretarial service and public relations office, owned and operated solely by Silvia Fitzpatrick.

After receiving her master's degree, Silvia joined the English department at the university. A teacher was a respected position. By the time Hallie entered high school they had a stable income and Silvia had met her goal. She was assigned to teach remedial students. And she found that she loved the challenge and relished her small successes. Her loose schedule fit well with raising her child and operating her business, and for the last four years that Hallie lived at home, they managed.

But Hallie's sudden decision at seventeen to marry a man who was going to play professional football had led to their first real quarrel. When Hallie rebelled by eloping, Silvia had been crushed. Everything else she'd been handed in life she'd handled. But Hallie, headstrong and in love, refused to listen to reason. From that day on, Sylvia swore that she'd never allow herself to lose control again. Up to now she'd managed. It was the terrible guilt she hadn't known how to deal with.

Nobody ever knew how alone she'd been when Hallie's young husband had immediately turned pro and moved them to California before Charlie was born. For Hallie's sake Silvia managed to pull herself together when John died, but when Hallie left ten years later, Silvia began the final construction of the walls of separation that protected her from ever being hurt again.

Then, a month ago, Hallie had unexpectedly appeared at her door announcing that she'd left her husband Jeff and was moving back home. Hallie hadn't given any explanation, and Silvia hadn't known how to ask. Assuming that they'd had some kind of spat, Silvia had accepted her only child back into her life temporarily.

"Don't interfere, Mother," she'd been told when she'd asked. "It's my problem and I'll handle it."

And Silvia hadn't known how to reach her daughter. She could only understand her pain.

Then Hallie had signed up for classes and Silvia realized that the separation might be more permanent. Now Hallie had brought home a Nightwing with wicked eyes and outrageous statements about making love. What was happening to Silvia's carefully organized life?

"Mother?" There was a knock on the office door and Hallie poked her head cautiously around the corner. "Are you all right?"

"I think so," Silvia said quietly, leaning back in the mauve-cushioned chair behind her desk. "You?"

"Mother, you don't have to be so blasted calm

about this. I thought I'd get back before Fletcher arrived. I was going to explain."

"I'm sure you were, Hallie. You always do."

"And you are upset, Mother. I can always tell."

"Oh? How? I'm certainly not screaming or insisting on explanations, am I?"

"No, of course not. You never do."

"I did once and I drove you away."

"Mother, Jeff and I already had the license. We were young, foolish. We thought his family would never approve of our marriage. We were wrong. They've accepted me fine. It was me, Mother, not you. You didn't drive me away."

"I didn't?" Silvia was stunned. Hallie was only saying that to make her feel better. She still remembered the awful, angry words and Hallie slamming out of the house.

"No you didn't. We just had a fight. All mothers and daughters fight, except us. You were always so blasted calm. Just like now. You're calmly sitting here at your desk in the dark, holding a quart of strawberry ice cream that is dripping down the front of your neat, efficient blouse."

"What?" This time Silvia didn't control her reaction. She came to her feet and looked down at herself in horror. Hallie was right. The ice cream that she didn't remember taking out of the grocery bag was making pink splotches down the front of her blouse and on her pale-green carpet.

"I'm sorry you're upset, Mother."

"You didn't upset me, Hallie. I . . . I can't imagine how this happened."

"Of course not. I'll bet you probably have a breath-stealing, heart-stopping, practically nude winged man putting your kitchen on sex alert every day."

"Hallie!" Silvia's response wasn't calm. It wasn't even controlled. She bit back the thought that her kitchen had probably never been on "sex alert" until now. "You're wrong about that. I never have, until you came home. Don't you think that you could have at least asked me before you invited Mr. Sims to move in?"

Why was she worrying about Hallie's not having called her after what she'd just learned? Because she'd learned to control her emotions too well. Except where this bug man was concerned.

"I tried, Mother. I called for over an hour, but nobody answered the phone. Then I had to go to class. You must have been shopping."

Silvia slid the wastepaper can under the ice cream and started back toward the kitchen, holding her breath as she stepped through the door. Empty. Thank goodness. She put the ice cream in the freezer and reached under the sink for cleaning supplies to attend to the carpet before the splotches had time to dry.

"What on earth made you think I'd want to rent the garage apartment, Hallie?"

"Well, I just thought that with Charlie and me here, we could use the extra money, at least until I get things worked out with Jeff. I'm sorry, I should have waited to ask you, but Dr. Evans was sure you'd agree."

"Hallie Fitzpatrick Warren wait? Why? You

never have before." This time her voice was intentionally sharp. She saw the wince that crossed Hallie's face and wished she could take the words back. She wasn't angry with Hallie, not really. Well, she was, but not about the garage. Her emotional outburst was because of that man and his sexual insinuations.

Silvia gathered her cleaning supplies and went back to her office. Hallie followed, watching for a moment as Silvia sprayed the spot with soil remover and began to blot up the ice cream.

"It seemed like a good idea at the time, Mom. I didn't realize that you'd be so upset. I'll tell Fletch that I made a mistake."

Silvia paused and looked up at Hallie's worried expression. "I'm sorry, darling. It's just that I never expected to rent out the apartment again. Your father and I lived there until his parents died. I only rented it out while you were at home because I needed the money. Nobody has lived there for years. I thought it might not look right to have strangers here when I was alone. Mr. Sims was certainly a surprise. Does he always dress like that?"

"Don't know. He looked pretty normal when I met him in Dr. Evans's office."

"What exactly does he do?"

"He's to be the writer-in-residence for this quarter. He just came in from some island in the South Seas expecting to find a room, and you know that it's impossible to find housing fall quarter. He's already a week late and there isn't a vacant room between here and Lawrenceville."

"Why doesn't he stay with Greg?"

"Mother, I hate to be the one to tell you, but I think that Dr. Evans has a lady living with him."

"Greg is living with someone?" Silvia couldn't keep the surprise from her voice. There'd been a time, right after Hallie had eloped, when he'd invited her out. But she'd refused, believing that a teacher shouldn't become too friendly with her employer.

Hallie smiled indulgently at her mother. "Then Dr. Evans remembered your garage and . . . I'm sorry, Mother. I guess Fletch was a shock to someone as sheltered as you are."

"Sheltered!" Silvia came to her feet and moved briskly back into the kitchen. She rinsed her cleaning cloth in the kitchen sink and glanced out the window. Was that what Hallie thought she was? The idea that everyone considered her to be some pure, protected woman who was out of touch with the real world bothered her terribly, and she didn't know why.

One thing she did know was that having Fletcher Sims as a faculty member was going to come as a shock to everyone on the staff. She wondered what they would think about his living in her garage?

The university always had an artist-in-residence program, though being involved in the remedial program she didn't often cross paths with them. Greg Evans was known for exposing the students to a wide variety of literature and writers. Still, she didn't think that Fletcher Sims was what the staff had expected. She wondered why he'd come here.

Silvia squeezed the cleaning cloth dry and glanced out the window. The kitchen window and Silvia's bedroom were directly across the yard from the garage apartment bedroom. Silvia didn't mean to watch. She'd never considered herself sheltered. The people who had watched her grow up would have laughed at the idea of Silvia the wild child ever being conservative. She'd worked hard at changing. And she had, so much so that she wasn't at all interested in the man who came into view in the uncurtained garage window.

Before she realized what she was seeing, Fletcher Sims threaded his long legs into a pair of jeans, pulled them lazily up his body, gave Silvia a jaunty salute, and slid the zipper closed.

Silvia gasped. The man had been totally nude.

"I know this is a shock, Mom, but are you all right?"

"No, I mean yes. Don't worry about Mr. Sims. We'll work out something temporarily until he can find another place. And, Hallie, I'm not so . . . unworldly as you may think."

Silvia knew that she was jabbering, a thing that Professor Fitzpatrick never did. "I mean I owe Greg Evans a lot. He keeps me on the staff when he could probably find someone else with better credentials. And he sends Options, Inc., a lot of business. Besides, where's my southern hospitality? It wouldn't be neighborly for me to turn Mr. Sims away. I'm just surprised that you're . . . interested in the man."

"My Lord, Mother, this is Athens, not Tara. Where'd you get that drawl. You sound like a cross between Melanie Wilkes and Mammie. I'm not interested in Fletcher Sims."

"You're not?"

"Heavens, no! Jeff and I may be separated, but until I work that out, the last thing I'm interested in is another man."

"I'm glad to hear that, Hallie. I'd hate to think that I'm a total failure as a parent."

"Failure? What on earth are you talking about?"

"Well, you've always followed in my footsteps, Hallie."

"Really? I've never considered us alike at all."

Silvia's eyes widened. They'd never talked about the similarities in their lives, but surely Hallie knew. "You don't have to pretend, darling. I married and had a child by the time I was eighteen and so did you."

"Yes, and you were a widow before you were twenty-five, a course I have no intention of following. That's why I came home, to make certain that doesn't happen."

"I don't think I understand."

"Maybe I'm wrong, Mother, but I'm gambling that I'm not."

"But you left your husband and now you've brought home a . . . very handsome older man. What am I to think?"

"Well," Hallie grinned, "I never considered it at the time, but after seeing the sparks between the two of you, if I brought Fletcher Sims home for anyone, Mother, it was for you."

TWO

Hallie took cleaning supplies and bed linens to the garage and by midafternoon the apartment was livable.

Fletcher returned Greg Evans's Jeep, grabbed a quick shower at Greg's apartment and hitched a ride, first to the State Patrol Headquarters where he got a temporary driver's license and then on to the motorcycle dealership where he bought a powerful red-and-black machine. By midnight, Fletcher Sims was more or less moved in.

By the next morning, awake and hungry, he was considering whether he wanted to match wits with his landlady in order to get a cup of coffee or whether he wanted to take a chance on a tent on the football field.

Silvia Fitzpatrick had turned out to be a pint-size, sloe-eyed angel with an icy gaze who posed as a Miss Manners lookalike and stared him down without flinching. She was faculty teas, the ballet in the spring, opera in the winter, and church every Sunday. Still, that polished demeanor couldn't quite mask the inner fire she was guarding. It wasn't the suave, man about-the-world Spider Malone who caught the force of her gaze. It was Fletcher Sims who felt the heat reach through the screen door between them and send unexpected danger signals down his spine.

Fletcher looked around the apartment and shook his head. Maybe the garage was a mistake. Surely there was something else in this college town. He'd slept places that didn't even have kitchens and showers. Forcing himself to face reality he decided that it wasn't the state of the apartment that was bothering him. It was his landlady.

Just take a respectable job for one quarter, rest a bit, and he was off again. That had been the plan. It wasn't the money. He'd spent little of what he'd earned in the last ten years. Hario Splendor was cheap living. A quarter on a college campus was to be a different kind of saving, saving Fletcher Sims. Here there'd be no wine, women, and song.

He was a writer with a sketchy reputation with his publisher, and, if the truth be known, fresh out of ideas. The last Spider Malone book had slipped a bit on the sales lists and it had been his fault. He was tired, burned out, brain dead for the first time in his career. He had another book due and he had no idea what it would be about. According to his agent the writer-editor relationship was badly in need of some sweet-talking attention, if Fletch ever expected a new contract.

Fletcher was sweating. He'd been cool enough, sleeping nude with all the windows open, but now the apartment was hot and it was only the middle of the morning. He staggered to his feet, leaned his head out the window and took a deep breath. If his landlady was watching, she could just get an eyeful. That's what his alter ego Spider Malone would say.

Fletcher shook his head. Why on earth did his mind keep coming back to Silvia Fitzpatrick? The last thing he was looking for was a woman, and certainly not one like her. He'd grown up with another Miss Manners and he still remembered feeling the wrath of her calm displeasure on the back of his legs and his bottom followed by the terror of being locked in a closet when a paddling wasn't enough.

The problem was that he had expected Silvia Fitzpatrick to be a typical small-town grandmother, a respectable pillar of the community living in a red brick house with masses of yellow chrysanthemums making a riot of color beneath her kitchen window. He'd promised Greg he'd behave. Silvia was a lady with a hand's-off sign written in invisible ink on her creamy skin.

And that was what was bothering him. At first glance she was perfect, with a mass of dark, rich hair, carefully cut in a swishy blunt cut that moved about her small porcelain face like a silk curtain. Her mouth was soft and pink, curling prettily over small white teeth in a frown that wasn't severe even when she intended it to be.

Fletch could deal with her dislike, even accept sharing her kitchen and her shower. The thing that didn't quite mesh in this quarter of solitude and good behavior he'd envisioned was the mental picture that flashed into his mind as he stood there trading quips with her on the porch—the very vivid picture of sharing the lady's bed.

Damn!

Fletcher Sims was not a happy man. Island hopping around the South Seas for the last five years had been free and wild, more than he'd expected and less than he'd wanted.

When his portable typewriter died, and an old tendency toward malaria flared up, Fletch gave in to his publisher's demand that he return to America where he could be reached by some means of communication faster than a banana boat. If the truth could be told, he was ready to come back to reality, to be a normal, everyday Joe Blow, to find out if the real Fletcher Sims still existed.

Feigning reluctance, he'd agreed to follow his agent's suggestion that he try living on a college campus as a concession to normalcy while he recharged his batteries. Athens wasn't too far from New York City to reach by plane if he became desperate enough, or Atlanta by bike if he wished. Perhaps this sabbatical wouldn't be a complete loss. By the end of the quarter he would be rested, fed up with rules and regulations, inspired and ready to go. When he turned Spider loose again, there'd be another best seller forthcoming.

Fletch pulled on a pair of cotton shorts and stepped through the window out onto the roof of the shed attached to the garage. Not a private porch, but it would have to do.

Automatically his eyes focused on the kitchen window, then traveled up to the bedroom above. The flutter of the curtain told him that someone had been watching him. Silvia. The shiver in his lower body said that he'd known it all along.

A child's cry broke the early-morning silence. The boy was unhappy about something. From the roof, Fletch watched as Hallie stepped out the kitchen door, Charlie under one arm and a load of books in the other. She laid the books on the top of the car and opened the door, feeding the unhappy boy into a car seat. His wail grew louder.

"Hey, what's the big guy's problem?" Fletcher hadn't known he was going to speak. He wished he'd kept quiet.

"He knows he's going to the campus nursery and he doesn't want to go. Mother has a business appointment and I have a class this morning."

Fletch caught the limb of the huge oak tree between the house and the garage and swung to the ground. "What's wrong with the nursery?"

From inside her bedroom Silvia watched the man walk over toward the car. This time she could see his strong face, dark brows, and spiky eyelashes. His skin was the color of mountain honey, warm and golden brown. He was barefoot again, no shirt, wearing another disreputable pair of cotton shorts. She'd better see what was happening.

Silvia pulled on her robe and started toward the

kitchen, reaching the porch in time to hear Hallie's explanation.

"Sorry if we disturbed you, Fletch. There's nothing wrong with the nursery. Charlie just isn't used to being left yet. Too many changes, I guess."

The man leaned inside the open window to talk to the child. "Hi, sport. You OK?"

The child had hushed and was sitting in the car seat staring at Fletcher Sims with a rapt kind of fascination. Silvia never expected the boy to hold out his chubby arms, asking to be taken. She never expected Fletcher Sims to oblige. Before anybody quite knew how it happened, Charlie was in her boarder's arms and Hallie was waving as she backed out of the drive.

This was too much. Silvia might have agreed to Mr. Sims' temporary stay in her garage apartment, but trusting her grandson to a stranger was something she couldn't allow. It simply wasn't . . . safe, even if he was Greg's friend. Silvia pushed open the screen door and stood on the steps.

"Mr. Sims? What are you doing with Charlie?"

"Well, as soon as I get dressed, we're going down to the campus grill and have breakfast."

"Going? How?" She'd seen him drive off in Greg Murray's Jeep and return on a great black motorcycle that shook her shower doors with the sound of its engine.

"On my bike, of course. Good morning, Mrs. Fitzpatrick. You're looking lovely this morning. I like a natural woman with skin that shines without makeup."

Silvia looked down at her pink satin robe hanging open and over the satin nightshirt she'd been wearing. Her face flamed and her stomach twisted as she realized how she looked standing outside her house completely disheveled. It didn't matter that she was still holding the wet washcloth she'd been cleaning her face with when she'd heard Charlie begin to cry.

Honey Watts's voice called out, right on cue, as always, "Something wrong, Silvia?"

"Now you've done it, Silvia," Fletcher said with a smirk. "We're caught in an indiscreet moment. Shall we give the old girl something to really worry about?"

Hastily, Silvia pulled her robe together. "No, Honey, everything's fine." She looped the ties firmly. "Forget that, Mr. Sims," Silvia said in a low stiff voice between lips clinched into a frozen smile. "We've already given the neighborhood enough gossip for the day."

"Well, you could give me a good-morning kiss."

"Kiss you? Are you mad? I won't allow you to put that child on a motorcycle. As for kissing you good morning, why would you even suggest such a thing? Bring Charlie into the house."

"Yes, ma'am. That might be a better idea. How about a cup of coffee, sport?" Fletcher followed Silvia to the porch, stopped and turned to face Honey West. "Honey, if you and I are going to get along, you're going to have to stop being so shy."

The silver-haired woman looked startled, then allowed a broad smile to move across her face. "Nothing shy about me, son. Come have lunch with me. We'll talk about Silvia."

"Fine. But I'll have to bring my friend, here."

"Sure, I've been trying to get Silvia to let me keep the boy, but they think I'm an old lady."

"Old ladies are like fine wine, darling—smooth, very smooth. Shall we say twelve o'clock?"

"Sure, and tell Silvia that my lips are sealed."

"Get in this house, and stop misleading my neighbor!" Silvia threatened with an unusual loss of control.

"Right away, Mrs. Fitzpatrick. I'd rather kiss you in private anyway." Fletcher switched the boy to his hip and caught Silvia in his right arm, pulling her close.

"What do you think you're doing?"

"Bug give Gran a kiss?" Charlie chattered happily.

"Bug isn't giving Gran anything," Silvia said sharply, struggling to pull away.

Charlie, sensing his grandmother's anger, began to whimper again.

"Now, see what you've done, Sylvia. You're frightening the child. Children need to be surrounded by love—lots of hugging and kissing. You should set a good example for the little fellow."

"But . . ." It isn't the little fellow who's doing the hugging and kissing, Silvia thought frantically as Fletcher Sims's eyes gave off wicked sparks and his lips descended. "This can't be happening," Silvia whispered, letting out a long, tight breath.

"It can and is. Don't you like being kissed, Silvia?"

"I don't know. It's been so long." Her lips parted involuntarily.

Then she knew. She liked being kissed, and very much. His lips were light and teasing, as if she were a sample being tasted by a connoisseur. She felt a tear somewhere deep inside, as though her heart had beat so rapidly that a tiny crevice had been ripped in its outer covering.

She allowed the kiss to go on a split second too long before she jerked away and leaned weakly against the kitchen sink. Fear fluttered through her, nudging her into a reality that she wasn't prepared for. This was a man, a real man who swooped down into her life with all the certainty of a small-town politician, knowing his appeal and exploiting it for his own gain.

Her breath was quick and uncertain as she raised her eyes to his. She'd expected him to be laughing at her confusion.

He wasn't.

She expected him to make some witty, sophisticated quip.

He didn't.

She expected him to be suave and blasé.

He seemed to be as surprised as she.

"Why?" she asked.

"I wanted to," he answered.

"Do you always get what you want?"

Charlie beamed happily and began to squirm.

Fletcher let him down and turned to face Silvia. "No, but I always go for it, even if I think the wanting might be a mistake. I think we need to try it again, Silvia."

"Don't be absurd."

"An action is absurd only when it's not committed honestly. I want to kiss you again and I think you want that, too."

Silvia swallowed hard, trying to still the jackhammer motion of her heart and her erratic breathing that seemed intent on making a lie of her words. "I don't kiss strange men, Mr. Sims. A kiss is a promise that I don't deliver lightly."

"Don't play games, Silvia. Don't kiss me if you choose not to, but don't lie about your desire. Words, feelings, wanting—those emotions are my stock in trade. You can't write about what you don't know. And I know when a woman and a man sing the same song."

Silvia tried not to feel the hard, firm flesh of his hip pressed against her body. "You're very sure of yourself, aren't you—coming into my house, forcing your way into my life with your charm and your . . . your maleness."

"Perhaps I am. Perhaps this is something new to me, too. But what I do know is that I'm rarely ever wrong about a woman. There's something here, whether or not we want it to be. You'll see."

Silvia looked down to where they touched, pink satin and rough cotton, hip to hip. Two incompatible fabrics made compatible by the mere touching of two even more incompatible bodies, and the invisible friction they were creating was undeniable. She forced herself to step calmly away.

"What I see is that you're full of yourself. I'm turning you down, Mr. Sims. Get used to it. There is coffee in the pot. You'll find bacon and eggs in the refrigerator. Use whatever you like, I have to get dressed. I'm expecting a client."

"Good idea, getting dressed. The only thing you're selling undressed is likely to be bought by me. I'm just not sure I can afford the price." Fletcher caught Silvia's elbow and turned her toward the door.

"Oh!"

"I warn you, darling, I'm an expert trader. You'd better get ready for a tough negotiating session." He gave her a quick kiss on the forehead and a familiar pat on the fanny that changed into a caress before she pulled away and ran up the steps.

The door slammed at the top of the stairs.

Fletcher rubbed the corners of his mouth with his thumb and forefinger. "Whee!" This wasn't working out the way he'd planned. His sojourn in the South was to be a period of rest and rejuvenation, not turmoil. This woman wasn't even the kind of woman he liked. He wasn't back on Hario Splendor where feelings were expressed freely, both physically and verbally. This wasn't the world of truth and beauty, and he wasn't looking for desire.

This was a college town in the fall, in a sheltered little corner of the world far away from full moons, hidden lagoons, and lovemaking on the sand. His body was making its own pictures, and the scene was bringing unbidden thoughts to his mind and stirrings to the part of him that had been put on hold. Damn, it was happening. He felt alive again, for the first time in too long. Why in hell did it have to be this woman?

He thought about the difference between the woman who had met him at the door yesterday and the peaches-and-cream woman he'd just kissed. The first Silvia was the lagoon, smooth and deep, like the beach at sunset after the tide had gone out, fresh and unmarked. She was a classy lady who needed a few ripples in her calm countenance. He'd just confirmed that the hint of fire beneath the surface was a raging bonfire.

Still, even he wouldn't have written such a scene. As a writer he'd long ago given up arguing with his editor about contrived situations. Life had a way of sending some real zingers. It was only in fiction that the plot had to be worked out logically. Life was clichéd, contrived, and unlikely. He knew; he'd lived every minute of his, damn the torpedoes, full speed ahead. He'd had no intention of slowing down, but he had—until now.

"Fwesh! Fwesh! Coffee for Charlie?"

The boy tugging on his leg was a welcome distraction.

"All right, Charlie boy, I'm starving. You and me, we've got some appetites to satisfy. Let's start with breakfast and see where it takes us. No coffee for you, kid. Sometimes a man has to redirect his hunger when what he wants is bad for him."

* * *

Silvia wished she weren't such a coward. She'd go back into the kitchen and insist that Fletcher Sims march over to the garage, pack up his things, including that ridiculous feathered mask, and leave.

She was a grown woman and she could handle herself. She refused to be intimidated or run over.

But this morning the distance between her bedroom and the kitchen might as well be a hundred miles. Her self-confidence might fool Hallie, but dealing with renegade students, demanding clients, and surly repairmen wasn't the same as a face-to-face confrontation with Fletcher Sims. He'd kissed her. She'd let him. She still wasn't sure how it had happened.

Even now she was staring into her mirror without a sign of emotion on her face. Anybody looking at her would never know that her stomach was tied in knots or that her heart felt as if it were a wind-up music box, jerking in an unfamiliar tinny rhythm.

When Hallie had married and moved three years ago, Silvia hadn't known how to let go of her restraints. She'd done that twice in her life with disastrous consequences. No matter what Hallie said, she'd never give in to her emotions again.

Her business, Options, Inc., had been an accident, or even a matter of luck. She had never set out to become a businesswoman. But then she'd never set out to be a widow before she was twenty-five, either. Work was safe. It could be controlled.

"Damn, you, John Fitzpatrick," she started to say, then swallowed her words as she realized that the man she was angry with wasn't her husband. John hadn't meant to crash his car into the tree that killed him. But he had, and now, all these years later the anger she'd submerged began to churn inside her. Until now the shadow of her husband had stood between her and other men.

In truth she could hardly remember what John looked like. He would forever be her first love, the father of her child, but now she was a woman. They'd lost their connection. Her childish outbursts of anger had been responsible for that and the guilt would always be with her.

Silvia backed up and sat down on her bed, biting her lip as she realized the awful, final truth. John was gone. He had been for a very long time. She couldn't change it then and she couldn't change it now. She'd lost everybody she'd ever loved, the grandfather who'd raised her, her husband, and finally her child.

Now a blue-eyed stranger had gotten past her defenses and set off all these unwanted feelings with one kiss. She was ashamed to acknowledge the excitement she felt.

No, she couldn't accept that. "Damn you, Fletcher Sims! This is all your fault. All your fault," she repeated in a whisper. Silvia didn't know how long she'd sat there in silence when there was a soft knock on her door.

"Silvia? Are you dressed?"

There was a second knock. The door opened and Fletcher Sims poked his head cautiously inside. "Oops, sorry. I thought you'd be ready by now. Your client is here. I showed him into your office and told him you'd be right down. Shall I keep him busy till you get there?"

"My client?"

Silvia stood up, looking at Fletcher, her face wooden until the reality of his words came crashing over her.

"Oh, my client. Now look what you've made me do. First the ice cream melted. Now . . . No . . . it isn't your fault. Thank you, Mr. Sims. I'll be right there."

Fletcher waited for another long minute, a puzzled frown on his face. Then he closed the door. She heard his jaunty footsteps as they danced down the steps. Like a grown-up Charlie, she thought, chastising herself for dallying when she had a business to run. She moved briskly toward her closet.

A few minutes later she'd donned a simple dark-green shirtwaist dress with a matching red-and-green print scarf that complemented her dark hair. She quickly applied light makeup, ran a comb through her shoulder-length blunt pageboy and threaded her small feet into brown low-heeled leather pumps. Taking a deep breath Silvia Fitzpatrick descended the stairs.

Charlie was busily smearing grape jelly on a piece of toast in the breakfast room. The door that connected Silvia's office to the rest of the house was ajar, allowing Fletcher to watch the boy at the same time he carried on a conversation with

Warren Middlebrooks, the business manager for recording artist and superstar, Kris Killian.

"Mr. Middlebrooks," Silvia said with a gracious smile. "I'm very sorry to have kept you waiting."

"No problem, Mrs. Fitzpatrick. I'm delighted to learn that Mr. Sims is here. He has suggested that he bring you out to Kris's ranch this afternoon so that you can get the full picture of the estate for your new campaign."

"Mr. Sims suggested that, did he? Well, I think the information and the pictures you've already supplied tell me what you want in the sales brochure."

"Nonsense, Silvia." Fletcher, who'd been propped against the front of her desk, came lazily to his feet to stand beside her.

"You know women, Warren. Silvia's just shy about meeting Kris. You don't have to worry, Silvie." He threw his arm across Silvia's shoulder and gave her a reassuring smile. "Kris is in L.A., making the arrangements for his next concert tour. He won't even be there."

Silvia shrugged and stepped away. "And neither will you, Mr. . . ."

"Oh, that's all right, Silvie, I don't have anything else to do. I understand that Kris has horses and a spectacular barn and show area."

"Indeed," Mr. Middlebrooks added, "not to mention tennis courts and a swimming pool. I hate to see him sell it. You know Kris. Buys a place, spends a fortune to fix it up, then he's off to another project. But then you know about that kind of life, don't you, Sims?''

"Oh, yes," Fletcher agreed. "I've done a bit of moving around during the last few years. If three o'clock suits you, Warren, Silvia and I will be there."

Silvia stood, listening to the two men make arrangements for her to accompany Fletcher Sims to the multi-million-dollar estate of her client, singer and actor Kris Killian. She might as well not have been there.

Once the door closed behind Warren Middlebrooks, Silvia turned to her boarder with more anger than she'd ever allowed herself to admit in her entire life.

"How dare you? How dare you interfere in my business with Warren Middlebrooks? Writing the brochure on this sale is the biggest job I've done and I will not allow you to sabotage it. I won't."

Silvia was trembling. Her voice was shaky and barely audible. She simply couldn't believe the man's audacity. Never, never had she met anyone like him. She was so angry that she couldn't even express it.

"Now, Silvia. You'd better sit still and let me explain what happened."

"Explain."

"Warren Middlebrooks came here with the express purpose of telling you that they had decided to give the brochure to an Atlanta firm. I introduced myself and somehow . . . somehow he got the idea that I was working with you. That seemed to give him second thoughts about his mission."

"You? Why on earth would he think that you are working with me?"

"I think it had to be Charlie. He told Warren that I live with his gran now. It seems that Warren is one of my most ardent fans. We share common tastes."

"You can't mean that he wears kinky costumes, too."

"No, he's an action adventure fan. He likes my books."

Silvia was beginning to get a bad feeling about what she was hearing. When she'd learned that he was to be writer in residence for fall quarter she'd assumed that he wrote fine literature. "I'm almost afraid to ask, Mr. Sims. What do you write?"

"Oh, don't be. I'm rather proud of how profitable my hacking around the world has become. I thought you knew. I write men's popular fiction."

"You write those sex thrillers about those awful Spider Malone kind of characters who search the world for adventure? I don't believe it. What can our students possibly learn from you?"

"Guilty. Fletcher Sims, the one and only, successor to Ian Fleming and Mickey Spillane. What they can learn from me, I can't imagine. It's Greg Evans's idea. You can ask him later at the faculty tea tomorrow. In the meantime, I suggest we make plans. By the way, you don't have to thank me, Silvia."

"Right," Silvia said with determination as she pushed her interfering boarder toward her door. "I don't and I won't. As for you, Mr. Fletcher Sims, I know enough about what happens in the kind of books you write. I have no intention of being associated with you."

"But, Silvia, think of the fun my women have. They travel the world, from the South Pacific to Saint Moritz living out every woman's most secret fantasy."

"Not mine, Mr. Sims. Now get out of here. You're supposed to be baby-sitting. Baby-sitters in this house are expected to be responsible for their charges."

"Not to worry, darling, Charlie and I will be fine. By the way, the women in my books positively adore," he held back the Spider Malone name, substituting instead, "my men of adventure." He slipped through the office door, holding it open one last minute while he added seriously, "Wear something casual, Silvia. I don't think we can muck about in the horse lot with you dressed like an English matron on her way to tea."

The paperweight that Silvia was holding hit the closing door, and she hadn't even known she was throwing it. How dare he? Barging into her home and taking over her grandchild was bad enough, but her life and her business? He'd kissed her, made her give in to her bad temper and . . . and . . . saved her from losing the biggest account she'd ever had.

The man wasn't Fletcher Sims; he was a real life adventurer. He didn't write fiction; he wrote his own autobiography. Honey Watts had dragged her to the movies to see all the those men of action films. She didn't have to read the books to know that Fletcher Sims and the character he wrote about were the same.

After an hour of pacing about, studying her proposal and checking her facts about the Killian property, Silvia admitted that Fletcher might have done her a real service. What she'd presented was shallow, a plastic, uninspired presentation of some rich man's plaything. There was no real life to it because she'd never seen the estate she was trying to sell. She was like Cinderella trying to re-create a fancy ball when all she'd ever seen was her stepmother's kitchen.

The Killian Ranch was isolated, expensive, and would be hard to market. The brochure Warren was ordering would be sent to foreign investors worldwide. It had to be something very special. Why hadn't it occurred to her to view the property? Fletcher was right. She needed to develop an on-site presentation. Still, making the trip to the ranch with Fletcher Sims? She'd squelch that right away.

But the kitchen was empty, as was the yard and the garage apartment. She didn't go inside, but with Charlie around she'd know if they were there. Where had they gone? It was lunchtime. Charlie would be hungry. Did Fletcher have any idea of what happened when a two-year-old got overtired?

A little after one, Silvia finally gave up her search and heated a can of cream of tomato soup. She was sitting at the breakfast-room table when she saw Fletcher through the hedge. He and Charlie were at Honey's house, having lunch on Honey's porch.

Silvia groaned.

This was a small university town. With Charlie announcing that Fletcher lived with his gran, it wouldn't take twenty-four hours for everybody in the community to know about Fletcher Sims. A reputation that had taken her years to build had likely already been destroyed and there was nothing she could do about it.

Rinsing her soup bowl, Silvia went into her office and put a Pavarotti tape on the stereo. The Killian Ranch wasn't her only account. She had other work. She didn't even want to think about how Fletcher Sims's presence would affect her professional reputation. What on earth was she going to do?

"Well, it isn't boots and jeans, but I guess that's as close as you could come." It was exactly two o'clock and Fletcher Sims was standing on the back porch, waiting.

Silvia jerked her eyes down to take in the slacks and jacket she'd chosen. "What's wrong with what I'm wearing?" Dark-blue and sharply creased, her slacks were matched with a blue-and-white-striped linen jacket and a red silk blouse, casual while still professional.

One look at Fletcher Sims and Silvia knew that he had taken his own advice seriously. His jeans were clean, but they were . . . The only word that came to her mind was "spectacular." They fitted his body like a second skin, riding low on his lean hips without looking in the least indecent. He wore expensive, scuffed reptile-skin boots. But the *pièce de résistance* was the hot-pink, oversize cotton shirt and the matching pink baseball cap advertising Bull Durham chewing tobacco.

"Wrong?" He shrugged his shoulders nonchalantly. "Nothing, if the members of the Ladies' Auxiliary were going on a field trip. For Kris Killian's ranch you might be a tad fussy. Still, it's your show, babe. Let's go." Fletcher pushed open the screen door and bounced down the steps.

Silvia followed him. "What do you mean, let's go? Where's Charlie?"

"Taking a nap at Honey's. She's going to watch him for us until Hallie gets back."

"Us? You are not accompanying me to the Killian Ranch." Silvia looked at the empty garage and down at her watch. Where was Hallie?

"You don't understand, Silvia, I'm not accompanying you. *You're* accompanying *me*. This trip isn't totally for your benefit. It's for me, too. If the reasons happen to overlap, all the better."

"How can anything you're involved in possibly overlap my meeting with Warren Middlebrooks?"

"Simple. You need me to get the contract, and I'm doing research for my next book. I'm thinking of using the ranch as the setting." He wasn't, but now that he'd mentioned it, the idea wasn't bad. "If you play your cards right, Silvie, I might make you one of the luscious nubiles in one of the bedroom scenes."

"Mr. Sims. I don't play cards. The last place I'd want to be is in one of your books. I'll get the contract on my own ability. And don't call me Silvie!"

"Ability has nothing to do with it, Mrs. Fitzpatrick. It's knowing how to play the game. I don't know why I'm surprised that you don't know how to play cards, Silvia. Other than word games, what kind of games do you like?"

Games?

Silvia stood her ground. She didn't take chances and she avoided dangerous situations that she might not be able to control. So what if she was standing there radiating sexual innuendoes? This was her company, her reputation at stake, and she wasn't about to allow some fast-talking game player to take over her life.

He dealt in words, spoken and mental. She knew that. She refused to see the bedroom scene he'd suggested. Never mind that her mind seemed to have been visited by his imaginary Nightwing forcing her, for one outrageous moment, to see herself in his arms.

Fletcher Sims wasn't real. She understood the man now. He was a doppelganger in reverse. Instead of being a shadow of a living person, he was a carefully drawn copy of the man of adventure he wrote about.

Silvia walked down the steps into the yard. "I'm not a game player and I have nothing in common with those women in your books."

Fletcher let his eyes catalog her appearance, carefully examining her shoes, her slacks, and the tailored jacket she was wearing. She was wrong about that. It was the red blouse that told him.

Even when she tried, the lady wasn't able to totally restrain that tiny wicked little part of her that responded to him. He cocked his head and pursed his lips as he studied her. Then he smiled, that lazy, knowing smile that threatened her resolve. The day was going to be fine.

"Oh, I don't know, Silvie," he finally said. "I think I'll reserve judgment on what kind of woman you are. Let's get going, shall we?"

"Where's Hallie? She should have been back by now."

"She called while you were listening to the maestro. I told her to take her time, that Charlie was taking a nap at Honey's and that we have an appointment. No point in her cutting short her studio time. We'll take my bike."

"We are not taking your bike, Fletcher Sims. You aren't going with me. This is business and you're . . . you're a distraction."

"Sorry, Silvia, it won't work." He lowered his eyes as though he regretted his insistence. "Whether you want me along or not, I'm afraid that I'm part of the deal. Warren made it very clear—no Fletch, no future."

This time there was no joking in his expression, nor in his tone of voice. Fletcher Sims was serious, too serious, and Silvia was beginning to get the message that if she intended to land this contract, she'd better put away her aversion to her boarder and take him along.

"All right, but we'll wait for Hallie to return. I don't intend to ride on that . . . thing."

"Come on, Silvia, get serious." Fletcher fell in

behind her. "Do you think that Fletcher Sims could drive up in a station wagon? Think of my image. Warren Middlebrooks is expecting a sophisticated man of action, not a bumbling character like that television detective, Columbo."

Silvia glanced at her watch and grimaced. If she didn't keep the appointment, she might lose the contract. Maybe Fletcher Sims was right. She was putting her own foolish pride ahead of her career. If Warren Middlebrooks wanted Fletcher, he'd get him. But she'd be the one to decide.

"Your image isn't the issue here, sport," Silvia said sharply. "I mean to land this job. Me—not Fletcher Sims. If I have to ride a wild mustang to get it, that's what I'll do. Let's get moving." With great misgivings she surveyed the huge black machine parked beside the wagon. "Are you sure that thing is safe?"

"Absolutely," Fletcher assured her. "I've had three lessons and the state of Georgia even gave me a license to drive it." With an infectious grin he backed the machine out, turned it around, and rolled it down the drive.

"Let's go."

"Just a minute," Silvia protested. "Where are the helmets? I refuse to ride without a helmet."

"Oh, yeah. I threw them in the garage somewhere. In California you don't have to wear these things." He kicked up the parking stand and walked back inside. Moments later he returned with two helmets.

"I thought these would be patriotic—red and black, Georgia's school colors, you know." He removed his baseball cap, folded it, and slid it into his back pocket.

"Yes, I know."

Silently, Silvia slipped the strap of her bag over her shoulder, fastened the helmet over her head, and walked over to Fletcher, who was now straddling the powerful machine.

"Hop on. High ho, Silvia, away!" He started and gunned the engine, waiting expectantly for her to slide in behind him.

Fletcher caught a glimpse of Silvia's expression of panic and began to have guilt pangs. He'd hoped to take a little of the starch out of Professor Fitzpatrick's ironing-board demeanor. He hadn't reckoned on her grim determination. Of course this was hard for her. He'd bulldozed his way into her life and shattered her calm into a thousand shards of uncertainties. He didn't even know why he was doing it.

She straddled the cycle, leaning forward to stretch her arms around him. "Like this?" Even without visors on their helmets, communication was cumbersome at best, and an exercise in contortion to even make the attempt.

"For a novice, it'll do." With a jerk, Fletcher roared down the drive, throwing up his hand in greeting to Honey Watts who was hanging out her upstairs window.

"Way to go, Fletch," Honey called out, giving him a thumbs-up sign as they passed by.

Silvia groaned silently. She soon lost the feeling in her fingers from clenching them so tightly around her tormentor. If any of the other neighbors saw her, it was a one-way exchange because Silvia's eyes remained permanently closed. Once they left the clogged university streets and roared out on the country road, Silvia cautiously opened one eye, then the other. She wasn't certain whether the rope-strangling feeling in her stomach was because of the drive or the driver.

"Thank goodness we didn't run into a car," she managed to shout, hoping that her comment would slow him down a bit.

"And we didn't hit any pedestrians, either." Fletcher turned his head and nodded in confirmation. "Unless you count the policeman who jumped out of the way at the corner of University and Old Galilee Road."

The policeman? At least it wasn't the Dean. Silvia tried to lean back. It was obvious that Fletcher Sims was mentally ill. No sane person would drive one of these machines.

Of course, no sane woman would be on one of them, either, not when she knew the driver was some kind of wild animal that flew into the face of danger. Fletcher Sims was constantly goading her. He must think that she was a certified wimp. Well, she wasn't. It was simply that she was practical, preferring her old, paid for, serviceable automobile, and her simple, old, comfortable lifestyle.

Silvia took a deep breath and tried to clear her mind. The leaves were beginning to turn. Though it was still warm, there was an elusive hint of fall in the air that swept over the expanse of the Georgia countryside. They burst into an open area where there were fields of dried corn stalks on one side and an expanse of cut hay, rolled into huge circles to be fed to the livestock during the winter. By that time the quarter would be over and her tenant would be gone. Hallie would have reconciled with Jeff, and Silvia's life would be back to normal.

Fletcher Sims might not know it, but if he considered her lifestyle to be that of a recluse, he was in error. She fully intended to prove to both Fletcher and Hallie that there was nothing wrong with her, or the quiet way she lived. If she had any intention of holding her own with Fletcher Sims, she'd have to let him know that she was not ready to be manipulated and directed. She was as tough as he was.

The fact that she was on a motorcycle for the first time in her life ought to prove that. Secretly, she had to admit that she liked the feel of crisp wind blowing through her hair, of flying through the sunshine like some kind of winged creature.

Overhead she could see a hawk, soaring through the sky, then diving into the fields where he snared a field mouse before disappearing from view. Fletcher Sims was like that hawk, she decided. He was a predator who couldn't be contained, or controlled. She would do well to keep her distance. But she refused to be afraid of the man.

Who was she kidding? She was scared silly. She was the field mouse and Fletcher was a man who didn't take no for an answer. She'd never met anyone like him before. She'd never before felt the strange twinges of confusion that came every time they touched. As for his kiss, she hadn't allowed herself to think about that—not once.

This would be the last time she allowed him to maneuver her. Once she got the Killian assignment she'd get the stove in the garage repaired. Then he'd have to stay in his quarters, away from her. She wouldn't allow him to tease her into letting go. The Silvia who was once wild and free had been harnessed long ago.

Fletcher took a quick backward glance and saw her stern expression. He grinned, leaned back, and yelled, "Don't worry, Silvia, you're doing great. I'm going to bring you back to life yet."

Silvia felt the muscles in his chest contract, strong and tight against the palms of her hands. His heart was thudding steadily and she imagined how surprised he'd be if she slid her fingertips beneath his shirt and touched him. What if . . . ? She shook her head in disbelief. She was fantasizing about touching Fletcher Sims's chest. Then she recalled what he'd said.

"Bring me back to life!" she yelled, then softened her voice deceptively. "I'm not dead, Fletcher Sims, and I wish you'd quit making fun of the kind of life I lead. I'm free and alone, just where I want to be."

It was a mistake to challenge him, to give him reason to turn his head so that she could look at him. She recognized the amused curl of his lips and the spark of devilment in his dark eyes, that said he knew what she was thinking. She could feel a definite change in the beat of his heart and a quickening of the rise and fall of his chest beneath the arm still circling him.

Silvia shifted her weight, feeling her face flush. She couldn't move any farther away, and staying this close was an unnerving sensation. Mental word games again. She was seeing herself kissing Fletcher Sims, and for just a moment she knew that he was seeing the same thing. "I am not alone by necessity, Mr. Sims, but by choice."

Fletcher caught the small, sharp elbow pressing into his hip bone and squeezed it. "Not anymore, Silvia Fitzpatrick," he yelled, slowing the machine as he threw caution to the winds. "Don't you know by now? You're with Spider Malone, and the Spider's caught you in his web."

THREE

"Spider Malone? Is *he* your man of adventure?"

Spider Malone, the island-hopping, man of action was rich, smart, and handsome, equally welcome in the boardroom or the bedroom and was flying through the Georgia countryside, being held in her arms.

She should have put it together at once. Fletcher Sims, creator of Spider Malone—no, not creator—Fletcher Sims *was* Spider Malone. Silvia gasped, drawing air into her oxygen-starved lungs as she considered her conclusion.

Unmistakably it was Spider Malone who was driving the powerful black motorcycle. Trying to be an impartial observer, she recognized that the ultra-conservative Assistant Professor Silvia Fitzpatrick was hugging a man who could likely talk his way into the arms of any woman in the United

States. His very name scattered her ideas so that she couldn't even begin to organize her thoughts. She was a lady of words and, for once, no words came to mind.

Silvia turned her head, focusing her attention on their route. She shivered. She wasn't riding in a truck, but she'd been down this emotional road before. There was one big difference, however. This time she wasn't seventeen.

Running along the road was a white fence caught up between brick posts like a Christmas garland. Beyond the fence were still green pastures, with fat lazy cattle on one side and sleek, powerful horses on the other. Several of the mares had colts, racing about the pasture like leggy children playing tag and chasing butterflies.

Fletcher slowed the engine and brought the cycle to a stop at an iron gate. "Hold the bike for a minute." He walked up to the column on the left and pressed a buzzer mounted in the brick. The gates magically swung open.

"Impressive, isn't it?" Fletcher was smiling as he walked back, threw his leg over the bike, and leaned his head back toward Silvia. "Well?"

She couldn't sit there like a stump and she wouldn't let him know what confusion his disclosure had wrought. Staying even with Spider Malone would be a challenge. But she'd met tough challenges before.

"Well?" Fletcher repeated, amusement lacing his voice as if he knew the battle raging behind her stern expression.

"Well, what? If you're waiting for me to be

impressed with your open sesame approach to locked gates, I'm not. If you're referring to the ranch, it's magnificent."

She responded too sharply. Let him think it was the fear of the unknown waiting ahead instead of a reluctant admiration for the man who was sweeping her up into one of the adventures he wrote about and the very real fear that she couldn't stop it from happening.

"No, I'm waiting for you to put your arms around me again. We're flying on wings of steel, Silvia Fitzpatrick, and you're the only thing holding us on the ground."

She was right to keep a sharp hold on her response. He was just a traveling man; he was a man accustomed to flying. She was a woman determined to keep both feet on the ground. Still, she admitted grudgingly that she could learn to like the freedom of speeding about the countryside.

"Your body may be earthbound, but your mind is in orbit, Spider Man." Silvia clamped her legs around the machine and braced herself into a forward-leaning position. "Let's get this crazy trip over with, Mr. Sims. I can handle it."

Silvia just managed to grab hold of his belt in the ensuing burst of force as the machine took a powerful jump and raced forward. She was holding on for dear life, her fingers clutching his belt, her thumbs stretched low inside his jeans, digging madly into bare skin. After a wild shot down the drive, he slowed their movement to a crawl and spoke over his shoulder.

"Much more 'handling it,' darling, and you're going to rip my pants off. It isn't that I don't like a little fooling around, but a motorcycle isn't the best place for it."

Silvia felt a flush of color move up her chin and flood her face. She slid forward, detached her fingers from his belt and clasped them around his chest. She was definitely agitated. There was no disguising her discomfort. One way or another she had to maintain some semblance of control in this venture. Taking the offensive in the classroom was her method of choice. Why not here?

"All right, you've proved your point. We both know that you're a man who insists on being truckled to. Does that make you feel macho?"

Fletcher felt the tension in Silvia's arms. He'd felt her take a deep breath and let it out again. Truckled to? Fletcher wasn't sure what that meant. But his actions didn't make him feel good at all. The kind of man-woman adventures he'd instigated a thousand times suddenly seemed out of place with Silvia, and he was ashamed.

Somewhere along the line, years ago, he'd merged himself with Spider Malone and he wasn't certain where the dividing line was drawn. The Spider Man persona was what the world expected and he'd become accustomed to satisfying the demands of his public. Now this woman made him examine his motives and that was more uncomfortable than he wanted to admit. He wasn't sure any more who Fletcher Sims really was.

Instead of answering her real question, he slowed the engine and brought them to a stop beside a large lake, where she could see the house. "I like being truckled to, huh? Truckled to? What the hell does that mean, Professor?"

"Oh? You agree that a lowly staff member of the English department knows a word your Nightwing hasn't planted in your head, Mr. Sims? Maybe your bird of words in the night needs to take one of my classes. Truckled is a verb that means to cringe and fawn, to yield to a superior being."

"Superior being?" Fletcher gave a wry smile. "Don't bet on it, Silvia. Still . . ." he paused, drawing out the thought as if he were viewing it for the first time, "maybe you're right about one thing. Maybe you've discovered the terrible truth. Maybe my Nightwing has deserted me in my hour of need and taken all my words with him."

The man sounded genuinely puzzled, not distressed, but sad. He wasn't wisecracking now. There was too much pain in his voice. Silvia couldn't figure him out. Every time she began to put a composite together, the man revealed some new, unexpected side to himself. Pain and regret seemed out of place. She didn't want to feel compassion, but she did.

"Does someone really live in a mansion like this?" Silvia asked huskily. She forced her attention on the Tara-like structure that caught the light like a white silk Oriental fan in the sunlight.

"Occasionally. I'm told Kris comes here when he wants to escape the mad rush of his show-business life in California. Brings ten or fifteen of his closest friends and plays for weeks, until he's unwound."

Silvia looked around. Behind the house were several barns. Off to the side were tennis courts, and gardens filled with fall-blooming flowers.

What she saw was a watercolor day. All the colors muted and blurred; the blue canvas of the sky with traces of white clouds softly smeared across it. Maple and oak leaves were strewn over the expanse of green lawn and pasture like confetti. The air was poignant with the promise of the season's change from the heat of summer into the cool of fall. The falling leaves were harbingers of winter, waiting patiently out there beyond the loblolly pines in the distance.

"But why? I can't imagine anyone ever wanting to sell such a beautiful place," Silvia murmured softly.

"Perhaps he can't live here anymore. Perhaps it takes more than success and beautiful surroundings to sustain a man. Perhaps he's lonely."

Fletcher's voice was low and strained. Silvia felt a tension wash across him. Lonely? Was loneliness a reality that he as a successful artist could identify with? Still another disturbing glimpse of the real man.

Silvia might have pursued the idea of a man being lonely in the midst of peace and beauty, but once more Fletcher brought the powerful machine to life, and they rolled around the house to a stop beside an Olympic-size swimming pool that extended into an opaque glass-walled room at the back of the house.

Removing his helmet, he crossed his leg over the handlebars and unfolded his long legs from the bike before assisting Silvia to dismount. At that moment a door slammed and they looked up at the lean, unshaven man who was approaching with his hand extended. "Fletcher Sims? Glad you're here, man. I'm Kris Killian and I'm one of your biggest fans."

"Kris Killian? We didn't expect you. Warren told us you were in California."

"I was, until I heard who we were going to be dealing with on the prospectus. Flew in this morning. Bring your lady and come inside."

Silvia removed her helmet, hung it on the handlebar, and approached the world famous singer-actor. "Mr. Killian, please let me introduce myself. I'm Silvia Fitzpatrick, the owner of Options, Inc."

"Eh, sure. If you're the Spider's lady, you're welcome. How'd you connect up with Fletch here?" Kris opened the glass sliding door and stepped inside, waiting for Silvia and Fletcher to follow.

"I didn't," Silvia corrected firmly. She had to stop this misunderstanding. She wasn't Spider's woman, or Fletch's lady. She was her own person, a businesswoman on a business call. "Mr. Sims is living in my garage apartment. He was simply kind enough to—"

"Wow! This is spectacular, Kris," Fletcher interrupted, standing in the center of the large glass solarium housing the indoor portion of the pool. "We could get used to this, couldn't we,

Silvie?" He gave Kris a big wink and laid his arm possessively around Silvia's shoulder.

"Stop it, Fletcher Sims! You're deliberately giving Mr. Killian the wrong idea," Silvia snapped and tried to shrug his arm away.

"Oh, that's all right, Silvia," Kris said as he stepped behind a wood-and-glass bar. "You don't have to explain. I've been known to have a private relationship with a business associate or two. What will you have to drink?"

"A glass of iced tea would be nice," Silvia answered, taking advantage of Kris's turned back to give Fletcher Sims a warning frown and remove his arm from its place around her neck. "About Mr. . . . Fletcher," she began.

"As a matter of fact," Kris Killian went on, "when I heard that Fletch here was a part of Options, I decided to forget about my attorney's advice to go with a New York firm. Anybody who can get Spider Malone in and out of so many close situations ought to be able to put together a sales pitch that will help me unload this place without too big a loss."

"I ought to tell you, Kris. Silvia is the brains," Fletch drawled, reclaiming his hold on Silvia's shoulder. "I'm just a . . . a runagate, adding a little of my adventurous spirit to her ideas, aren't I, darling?"

"A runagate?" Silvia repeated, properly distracted by his statement as Fletcher had intended. She forgot to react to his arm around her as she searched her memory for the meaning of Fletcher's reference. It galled her to admit that she didn't know the phrase.

"A runagate, my lady of words. A runagate—one having no permanent home, given to wandering."

"That's us," Kris spoke up. "Runagates, both of us. We ought to get on just fine, Fletch."

When Fletcher nodded his agreement to Kris Killian, Silvia told herself three things. First, that Fletcher Sims was only playing the role that was expected of him. Second, that this outrageous exchange was only for the benefit of landing Kris Killian's job. And third, that the prickling sensation radiating beneath his touch was from pure anger, her anger—not the man's touch.

Silvia quickly decided that Fletcher Sims and Kris Killian were cut from the same mold. Both radiated the easy sensual power of men who were sure of themselves. Women probably hurled themselves at both Fletcher and Kris. Attractive, willing women, not women like her. She was simply the woman who happened to be here with Spider Malone.

Silence fell across the room for a long minute. Subconsciously she could hear the tinkle of glass as Kris filled glasses and poured liquid inside. Silvia weighed her choices. She couldn't allow the deception to continue. Even if the truth meant losing the biggest business opportunity of her life, she wouldn't play word games with a sex symbol, or sex games with a man of words to secure a contract.

Silvia didn't try to hide from Fletcher Sims the

argument she was waging with herself. He had to realize that she couldn't lie. Misleading a client was foreign to her very nature, and whether he approved or not, he had to accept her honesty. She saw the truth dawning in his eyes, followed by a sheepish grin that admitted regret for ever trying to force her.

"Tell him the truth, Mr. Sims," she said.

"If I must," Fletcher said reluctantly as he squeezed her shoulder painfully.

"Either you do it, or I will."

"Truth time, Kris. As much as I hate to admit it, Silvia and I don't have anything going here. We're not even business associates. She's just my landlady. I let Warren assume that I was working with her. I'm not. If you want to call off the deal, we're out of here. But I'd consider it a personal favor if you'd give her a chance."

Kris took a long, disbelieving look at Fletcher, then pursed his lips sternly. He took a long sip of his drink and grinned. "What the hell, Fletch? If I hadn't taken chances I wouldn't have made my first hit record. Let's just say, from one runagate to another—you owe me one, man—"

"Mr. Killian," Silvia interrupted. Whether or not she got this job was going to depend on her presentation, not on a personal favor to some bird man straight off a banana boat. "I appreciate your offer, but I'd rather you deal directly with me. If that's going to be a problem, I'll just say goodbye."

"Leave? No, I think I like somebody who is honest with me. That's rare. If it's truth time,

70 / ALLIE JORDAN

Silvia, then let's deal. I'm no superstar. The truth is, I'm just plain old Peter Killian from Boston, Mass. Quit high school and left town with a band when I was fifteen. Still have a mother in Worcester and a sister who's an artist in Rockport.

"That's my truth," he continued. "About yours, I think you're both wrong. There's something between you two, whether or not you know it yet. I can feel the vibrations, even if you don't. Now, do you want the guided tour or would you rather poke about here on your own?"

Fletcher answered for them. "Either way, Kris. By the way, I hope you won't mind if I use this spread in my next book." Fletcher picked up the two glasses of iced tea and handed one to Silvia. "This is a perfect setting for Spider's next adventure."

"Not if you write me into the story, and let me be in the movie," Kris said with enthusiasm. "If you don't mind, why don't you two just wander around. I have to make a few phone calls. When you're finished, we'll take a swim and grill a steak."

Fletcher put his hand on Silvia's back and directed her away from the pool. "Dinner sounds good. It's been a while since I've eaten good old steak and potatoes. A swim sounds great, too. The lady and I accept."

Silvia held back her reply until Kris was out of hearing range. "I can't stay here all afternoon," Silvia said angrily. "How dare you accept for me! I thought we'd settled that. Can't you be around a woman without implying that you . . . that you and I . . ."

They were walking along a marble foyer, through the great formal dining room, into a surprisingly warm and comfortable kitchen.

"Hush, darling. Kris might give a good businesswoman a chance, but I don't think he'd take kindly to dealing with a shrew." Fletcher took the glass of iced tea from Silvia's hand and placed it, along with his, on the kitchen counter. He took her hand as if he wanted to make a point.

Fletcher was a toucher. He'd always been a toucher and it seemed natural to hold her hand and turn her to face him. He hadn't intended to annoy her by accepting for her. Being in charge and giving flip responses was so ingrained in his lifestyle that they slipped out automatically.

"I'm sorry," he said softly. "I'm also curious. Which part bothers you, Lady Silvia, my accepting Kris Killian's invitation for you, the assumption that you're somebody's lady, or that you're mine?"

Silvia stared at him, wondering if he was deliberately trying to shock her or if this was part of his automatic come-on to the women he met. Then he smiled that slow, regretful smile that was so revealing and she knew it wasn't any of those things that had unsettled her.

Fletcher Sims had a stern, chiseled face with features that made him appear permanently angry. Yet, when he smiled his eyes lit up and therein lay the secret of his appeal. His eyes were wicked one minute, ashamed and contrite the next. She wasn't totally naive. She knew about masks and how easy it was to wear one. But looking at the man holding her hand, she sensed that there really was something hurting beneath his man-of-the-world exterior.

"You bother me, Mr. Sims. Who exactly are you and why are you here?"

"Who do you think I am?" He slid his fingertips up her arm to her cheek. His touch was as feathery as that of the Nightwing he'd described while he was standing on her porch yesterday morning. That meeting seemed to have happened a lifetime ago. Now his eyes bore into her, delving, almost hostile in their intent. He was forcing her to consider his question, yet she had the distinct impression that he was no more happy about what was happening between them than she.

Fletcher wasn't just a free-spirited, swashbuckling adventurer. He wasn't just a world traveler who also happened to be a famous writer. He wasn't even a winged creature who'd strayed from a South Seas island. To hang any of those tags on him would be to do him an injustice. But the true man was such a shadow figure that she couldn't define him yet. So she was driven to the same kind of flippant response that he'd used.

"I know what you are, Fletcher Sims," she whispered huskily. "You're bumptious. That means—"

"I know—'presumptuously insensitive and noisily self-assertive.'"

"Exactly. You seem to think you're some kind of island god and you're trying to cast a spell.

Well, it won't work. You'd better be careful that you don't get caught up in your own magic."

Tell the woman she's wrong, Fletcher pled with himself. *Tell her that this little interlude wasn't planned, that you're as surprised by your actions as she is.*

Casting a spell on Lady Silvia Fitzpatrick wasn't on Fletcher's rest and relaxation schedule. In fact, for the last year he'd run out of seductive steam. The truth was, he hadn't pursued a woman of any kind for longer than anyone would believe if he'd confided in them. There'd be occasional offers, for old times' sake, by the island women who cared for him and were worried about his unnatural celibacy. But he'd turned them down and there'd been no new conquests on the horizon.

Fletcher Sims had thought that he was getting old, tired, and burned out. A medical checkup had cleared him, except for an occasional flare-up of malaria. The doctor had agreed with Fletcher's self-diagnosed burn-out, though he'd laughed at the idea that a man could overdose on sunshine, sea islands, and women. Fletcher could have told him that even beach bums could have too much pleasure and that a piece of driftwood would eventually disintegrate if it didn't come to rest.

Now, in the space of two days, everything had changed. He wasn't burning with infatuation, it was more a feeling of anticipation. He was being challenged by a beautiful, stiff-necked grandmother with a grown daughter, and a grandson who called him Fwesh. Voodoo? No, though he recognized that a spell was being cast over him, a spell of home, motherhood, the flag, and apple pie.

"Of course, I'm a god, on a secret mission," he quipped haltingly. "I'm . . ." He searched for a word, but nothing came to mind. She'd scrambled his thought processes. The best he could do was, "machinating some evil scheme. Machinating is a verb meaning to—"

" 'Scheme or contrive,' Mr. Sims. I know. I wish that you wouldn't continue to challenge me. I wish you wouldn't touch me, either."

"Ah, I'm sorry, Silvia." Fletcher cautiously slid his hand from her cheek and pulled her close to him. "Let's stop spitting at each other. You want the truth? I didn't count on you, either. I sure as hell didn't plan to— Ah, forget it, we're just two people caught up in a situation that we can't do much about. Let's just try and work through whatever this is."

Silvia took a deep breath. For a long moment she allowed her face to rest against his shoulder. This was crazy. She was letting him hold her. The pink shirt he was wearing smelled like island flowers and sunshine. Being close to him, she conceded, felt, not good—but right.

"Fletcher . . ." She pulled away, took a deep breath, and stared at him. "I don't understand what is happening and I don't want you to make more of today than you should. This is a business appointment and a temporary assignment for you. Anything else between us would be totally insane."

"I know. You're right." He took a step back and caught her hand. "But do you suppose that we could forget for one afternoon that I'm a stand-in for Spider Malone and that you're Professor Silvia Fitzpatrick? As crazy as it sounds, I'd like to get to know the real Silvia."

"Why, Fletcher?" With knees dissolving into wet noodles, Silvia was standing in the kitchen of a mansion, far away from the university rules and regulations she'd abided by for what seemed like most of her life. That in itself was disturbing. To add to the fantasy, she was being held by a legend, who played with words and seemed to want to be a mortal man. Honesty? The truth was that she wanted to move back into his arms and feel their strength around her again.

"Why? Damned if I know," he said. "I just like the idea of Silvia being Fletch's lady for an autumn afternoon. I think it was Henry James who wrote that the loveliest words in the English language were 'summer afternoon.' He was wrong."

Fletcher leaned down. His hands were trembling. In another minute he'd be kissing her. No, it wouldn't take a minute. Their lips were already touching. This time, it wasn't just a simple meeting of two lips. This time, for one surprising second, the lady Silvia parted her lips in sweet, shy response.

"Oh, oh, sorry, Fletch." Kris came into the kitchen and stopped sharply. "But I've had to put my California calls on hold until later. In the meantime, I thought I'd take you around the ranch—unless you'd rather be alone."

"No!" Sylvia said, embarrassment choking off her voice as she jerked away from Fletcher. What was she doing, kissing the man, when she'd just insisted that he stop suggesting that they were having a relationship? She bit back unwanted tears of anger—not at Fletcher, but at herself.

For years she'd been too busy learning to support herself and Hallie to even think about men. She'd loved one husband and lost him. Afterward she'd made up her mind that she wouldn't take a chance on going through that kind of hurt again. Then one day she'd looked up and realized she'd forgotten how to be with a man. Hallie had built a life of her own, and Silvia was alone.

The dates she accepted turned into safe friendships rather than romance. Directing her energy into her teaching and her business, she'd thought she had everything she'd ever need. Now Fletcher Sims had come along with copious amounts of the one thing she was lacking—worldly experience.

"Great!" Fletcher agreed with Kris's suggestion for a guided tour, stepping smoothly away from Silvia. He shielded her flush of embarrassment by asking Kris about the tennis courts.

For the next hour Silvia worked through her confusion by taking prodigious notes of the facilities, the land, and other facts she already had back in her office in town.

Kris and Fletcher refused to leave her out of their conversation. By the time they returned to the house, Silvia was comfortable with the superstar of the recording and movie world. The fact that Fletcher cast secret glances toward her when Kris's back was turned only added confusion to the myriad complex of her feelings.

"What do you think, Silvia, can you write me a brochure spectacular enough so that we can unload my ranch on some oil sheik with big bucks?" Kris asked as they stepped back into the air-conditioned solarium.

"I'm sure I can, but I can't believe that you'd give up a place like this? I can tell that you love it."

Kris turned on a panel of recessed lights that turned the pool into a sparkling fairyland. Another flick of a switch and the glass walls closing off the outer edge of the pool slid open bringing the view of the sun setting behind the trees inside.

"You're right," he said sadly. "I do, or I did. When I built this, I thought that someday I'd marry. This was to be my safe hideaway from the world."

"What happened?" Fletcher sat down on an overstuffed white cotton couch and drew Silvia down beside him, making no move to let go of her hand.

"Nothing that hasn't happened before," Kris said too brightly. "This isn't the first hideaway I've bought, built, and sold. Finding a soulmate is harder than building safe havens. Would you two like a swim while I try that California call again?"

"No," Silvia said quickly.

"Great," Fletcher replied at the same time.

Kris looked at both of them with a smile.

"Look in the cabana, you'll find plenty of suits to choose from. We'll grill steaks later, if that's

OK with you guys. When I come here I try to live like ordinary people.''

"Ordinary people?" Silvia laughed lightly, looking around at the pool and the adjacent Arabian tent Kris referred to as a cabana. "Yes. I can see that."

"Yes," Fletcher echoed, drawing Silvia to her feet. "Ordinary people just like you and me. You find a suit, Silvia, and I'll use Kris's phone."

"Phone. What for?"

"To call Hallie, and let her know that we'll be home late. Wouldn't want her to worry, would we?"

Fletcher left to call Hallie. It was Fletcher who was concerned that somebody might be worried about them when the thought had never crossed her mind. Silvia found a light switch inside the cabana and looked around. The Arabian tent was divided into a lounge with a kitchen and two bedrooms. Kris was right. One bedroom was furnished with men's clothing and the other with a wide selection of women's suits—if the women were either size five or belonged to a nudist colony. Silvia decided that her underwear covered more of her body than one of these swimsuits.

"Find anything, Silvia?"

Fletcher was standing in the doorway behind her.

"Fletcher, I think I'll just watch you swim."

"Why? Don't you know how? I'll teach you." He was leaning against a pink pole that held up a swatch of fabric which could be draped to close off the doorway.

"It isn't that," she replied miserably. "It's . . . I mean, I can't possibly wear any of these suits."

"Mmm," he agreed, picking up a bright pink garment that was little more than two triangles of fabric. "This might be a tad skimpy, but I like the color. It's hot."

At the shake of her head he unfolded the next garment from the stack, a silvery-white one-piece swimsuit that had a loosely gathered swatch of material attached to a pair of briefs. "Says one size fits all, Silvie. What about it? It's regal enough for a queen and virginal by comparison."

"No. I mean yes. That one looks fine. The men's suits are in the room across the lounge. I'll meet you at the pool. Hallie and I took lessons at the YWCA when she was a little girl. I didn't want anything to happen to her."

She was jabbering. Anybody who could dive into a lake from twenty-five feet ought to be able to handle a swimming pool. Back then she'd been wearing shorts and a lot more clothes than this skimpy silver swimsuit.

Once Fletcher left Silvia tore off her casual, executive suit with the red blouse. She forced her lower body into the one-size fits all suit and wondered who was kidding who? It might not be skimpy, but the Spandex material fit like a second skin.

Although the upper portion of the material adequately covered her body, the lower half was cut in deep vees almost up to her waist on the sides. There was no mirror. Silvia was glad. She hurried.

She didn't dare take any chance that Fletcher would volunteer his help again.

As she dressed she faced the realization that her contract with Kris Killian was, whether or not she wanted to admit it, contingent on Fletcher's association with Options, Inc. Anything more personal was simply out of the question. For the sake of good manners if nothing else, she'd go along with Fletcher's plans for tonight. Tomorrow all that would have to end. He might think that he wasn't Spider Malone, but she wasn't sure of that at all.

Nervously Silvia listened. The last thing she wanted to do was let Fletcher get into the pool before her. If she were already there it would give her a kind of one-upmanship. Silvia walked to the diving board, took a deep breath, and dived in. The water was refreshingly cool as she came to the surface.

The hands that grabbed her waist from behind weren't cool at all. She didn't want to be turned around and caught in Fletcher Sims's arms, but outside of a struggle which would likely drown her, she didn't seem to have any choice.

His thick, dark hair was swept back by the water, forcing her to take a deep open look into eyes that were now heavy-lidded and mysteriously veiled. Beads of water spiked his lashes and caught the reflections of the pool lights like liquid silver. They weren't on some South Seas island, but they could have been.

"Hallie says that you should have a good time and she'll see you in the morning."

"In the *morning*. Surely you didn't tell her that

I was spending the night with you, I mean, *here*, did you?"

"No, that was her idea. You have a very worldly daughter, Mrs. Fitzpatrick. I told her that I'd have you home at a respectable hour, and we'd both wash her mouth out with soap for the naughty suggestions she made."

Silvia watched the water moving in great diamond patterns of blue and silver, sloshing them up and down, forcing their bodies together and away again. The situation was explosive and Silvia knew that she had to put some space between them.

"Please, don't make this any harder than it is."

"Too late, Lady Silvia." Fletcher pulled her close against him. "I couldn't stop that if I tried."

Silvia gasped. The obviousness of his reply pressed against her. "Fletcher! How can you even suggest such a thing?" She jerked herself out of his arms and swam toward the side, pulling herself lithely out of the pool and staring down at the man in the water below.

"A woman after my own heart," Fletcher agreed seriously and climbed out.

"What do you mean?" Silvia watched Fletcher leave the pool, cutting her eyes away from the visible sign of his desire. A towel, they needed towels. She remembered seeing stacks of them inside the cabana doorway.

"I prefer privacy, too." Fletcher was following her.

"This has gone far enough. We are not going

to . . ." She took a deep breath and turned to face her tormentor.

"To what, Silvia?"

He wasn't laughing at her. He was serious. He wanted to make love to her and he didn't care who was watching or how she might feel. The man was blatantly aroused and not in the least ashamed of it. And she was obviously unable to control what was happening with a simple refusal. This wasn't the kind of comfortable date she'd had with an old friend. She was hopelessly out of her element.

Normally she would have countered a student's challenge to her authority by fighting fire with fire. She'd have gone on the offensive and dared him to outthink her, or outdebate her on the rights or wrongs of their disagreement. Perhaps that would serve her in this instance also.

"Stop this, Fletcher," she said firmly, walking backward as she marshaled her rebuttal. "I realize that what we have here is a strong sexual attraction. I'm not going to deny that, but we must be sensible. You and I don't belong together. I don't have relationships. We could never be soulmates and it would be a mistake to even consider it. I won't, I mean, I don't want to make love to you."

"You're lying, Silvia. Your body wants mine just as mine wants yours."

"No . . ."

"Oh yes it does, darling. Look at yourself."

Silvia followed the line of his vision and gasped. The suit she'd thought so concealing inside had simply disappeared when it got wet.

Her full breasts were extended and perfectly outlined beneath a sheath of transparent silver that couldn't begin to conceal the dark aureole and throbbing nipples forming small pink buds beneath his gaze.

"You nursed Hallie, didn't you?"

"Yes. How did you know?"

"The breasts of a woman who's nursed a child become full and exciting. You're very beautiful, Silvia. You know that I want to make love to you. What you don't know is how important my wanting to is to me."

"Fletcher, I'm flattered. Nothing like this has happened since John. I . . ." Her voice trailed off. "I can't, Fletcher. This is easy for you. You probably won't believe it, but I haven't been with a man since my husband died. Loving a man is both a risk and a commitment, a commitment that I don't want to make. I think that I want to go home."

Never in his life had Fletcher wanted to love a woman so badly. And never in his life had he realized how much courage it took to say no. Silvia was right. She was a woman who needed a commitment. That was both her charm and her anchor. He was a man who couldn't offer her the future she needed and that self-knowledge was his anchor, different perhaps, but just as strong.

"You're right, Lady Fitzpatrick. Let's get dressed. We'll eat those steaks Kris promised and go home."

Kris was a charming host. He amused them with stories about his concert schedules and his movies, never quite concealing the lingering sadness in his life. Fletcher returned Kris's honesty with tales of his travels. He understood Kris's cynicism and the reason why he was going to sell the ranch. This beautiful haven represented Kris's failure—the loss of the thing he wanted most: marriage and a family.

"You're right, Kris. Soulmates are hard to find."

"Yes," Kris agreed, and Fletcher hadn't realized he'd spoken aloud. "You can always lose yourself in your books, Fletch. If you want something, you can have Spider figure out a way to get it. That must give you some pleasure."

"I suppose. But you know, sport, there comes a time when you have to get real. And reality is pretty cold and lonely, even if you're in the middle of the Caribbean."

It was late when Kris walked them back to the bike. He would be leaving for the Coast the next day, but they made a date to join him in his private box at the first home football game.

The ride back to town was dark and quiet. The sound of the motorcycle intruded on the silence of Silvia's neighborhood as they drove behind the house. She quickly unsnapped her helmet and slid from the back of the bike, anxious to get inside.

"Good night, Mr. Sims—" she began formally.

"Sweet dreams, Silvia," he interrupted hoarsely.

Silvia started toward the house, fumbling awkwardly in her shoulder bag for her key. She stopped and forced her fingers to relax so that she could find it. She'd simply been on a business appointment, nothing more. In the morning she would go to class and everything would return to normal.

Then she heard a sound behind her.

"Ah, hell, Silvie, I'm sorry, but if I don't kiss you good night out here I'm going to climb that tree outside of your window and come inside."

Later Silvia wasn't sure who closed the distance between them. All she knew was that he was kissing her, in full moonlight, by the corner of the porch in her own backyard. And she didn't know whether it was a dream or the fantasy of a voodoo spell. Her breath stopped, her lips parted, and their kiss deepened, carrying her into a place where her body recognized its own demands and refused to listen to any reason.

She came to her senses in time to realize that her hips were pressed against Fletcher in a shockingly intimate way and that Honey Watts's bedroom light had gone suddenly dark.

"Fletch, no! I . . . I can't." She pulled herself from his arms and dashed up the steps, making an attempt to smooth her blouse back in place as she frantically jabbed her key in the lock.

"Mother? Is something wrong?" The kitchen door swung open, throwing a circle of light across Silvia's unsettled entry.

"No, everything's fine, Hallie." Fletcher's voice came from the darkness beyond. "Your mother hasn't quite got used to riding a motorcycle. She's afraid the neighbors might get the idea that she's not the prim and proper professor they believe her to be."

"Everything's fine, Hallie," Silvia managed to whisper as she pushed her way past her daughter, valiantly ignoring both Hallie's raised eyebrows and Fletcher Sims's honest answer. "At least it will be, tomorrow."

"Close your window, Silvia," Fletcher called out. "You never know what kind of things fly about in the dark of the night."

Fletcher began to whistle as he crossed the back lawn to the garage, pausing for a moment when he reached the steps.

Silvia was halfway through the kitchen when she heard him call out, "Good night, Honey. By the way, I like my eggs scrambled for breakfast."

FOUR

"Ah, lady, don't hassle me. I don't need this," the tall, gawky student said, slumping forward in order to lay his head on his desk. "I'm just gonna play basketball long enough for the pros to scout me. Then I'm out of here."

The first weeks of the quarter were never smooth for Silvia, but this group of students was more unruly than most. Her classes consisted of general remedial students trying to make up what they hadn't learned in high school, athletes who often needed basic skills and disadvantaged students admitted on a trial basis.

As always, the problem was twofold—one of motivation and dedication. She was into the second week and it was obvious that this group was sadly lacking in both areas. Their lackadaisical attitude was revealed by total disinterest and outright rebellion when she collected their first homework assignment—a simple one-page statement of why they needed an education.

Of fourteen students, only ten had made any attempt to comply. The other four—two of the football players and two basketball players—had ignored their assignment completely.

"Maybe you will play pro ball." Silvia glanced at her class role, identified the belligerent basketball player as a city kid from south Atlanta and called his name. "Mister? Is your name really Mister?"

"Yep, my mama said that way I'd always get respect. She fixed it so that everybody had to call me sir."

The boy craned his neck, daring her to voice an objection. She had to admire the boy's mother. She had tried to instill pride in her son. Too bad she hadn't been able to help him learn how to earn it.

"Your mother was right," Silvia said, "but what happens if you don't make it as an athlete? What will you do then? How do you expect to get a regular job?"

"I ain't never gonna get no regular job, lady. I already know that, and nothing you try to teach me is gonna change it. I ain't gonna be cooped up in no factory building cars, or frying hamburgers at Mickey D's like my brother. I'm gonna see the world."

Silvia sighed. She'd run into this attitude over and over again. Likely the boy couldn't read. He had little knowledge of grammar and was embarrassed to admit he needed help, or accept it when offered. Without Mister's cooperation she'd never reach him. He'd already set himself up as the class leader. If she lost him, the others were lost, too.

Still, there was something about Mister Raschad. There was a swagger in his step, a chip on his shoulder, and a dare in his anger. He reminded her of Fletcher Sims—prickly yet vulnerable. He was a challenge, and Silvia didn't give up easily. She sensed that the boy knew he needed her help, but the last thing he would do was admit it.

Fletcher Sims. Every move she made brought her thoughts back to him. She hadn't seen him when she left this morning. His motorcycle had still been in the garage and his apartment was silent. The fact that she'd left an hour earlier than usual might have accounted for her missing him.

When she'd agreed to his staying, she hadn't considered that they would be sharing the same breakfast table and then leave for work at the same place at the same time. She hadn't seen Fletcher's schedule. Normally guest teachers might be assigned a small number of handpicked students, but the rest of the time would be given over to one-on-one meetings, guest lectures, and floating from one classroom to the other. She couldn't imagine what the students could possibly learn from a man who wrote spy stories.

It was after lunch when she looked up to find Greg Evans standing in her office door.

"Silvia, I just wanted to thank you for giving Fletch a place to stay. I know it was short notice, but I knew I could count on you. Having him here is important to me."

Silvia's words of denial died in her throat. He knew she couldn't refuse his request. But she could voice her concern over what he expected to gain by bringing a writer of men's adventure fiction on campus.

"Unfortunately the apartment isn't in very good shape. The stove needs to be replaced. Perhaps Mr. Sims would be more comfortable somewhere else."

"Nonsense, Professor Fitzpatrick." Fletcher stepped into the hall behind Greg. "I'm very pleased. Besides, since we're going to be working together, it will be easier."

"Working together? What does he mean, Greg?"

"Well," Greg answered. "I've felt for some time that we've neglected a large segment of our student body with our guest-artist program."

Silvia was getting a bad feeling about what she was hearing. "I don't understand."

"It's like this, Silvia." Fletcher's voice was suddenly not only businesslike, but sincere. "Anybody can stimulate the gifted students, but what about the misfits, the dropouts? Who stimulates them?"

"Probably nobody. But I'll play along. Who?"

"Me, the man who has been where they are now and still became successful, the man who couldn't spell, and learned to write books. Those kids need to know that nobody really lives a Spider Malone life except in the movies, but they can come close, if they really want to."

"What exactly does all this mean, Mr. Sims?"

"It means, Professor, that I'm going to be

working with your remedial students. I'm the example of what an ex-illiterate can do if he wants to live the good life."

"Absolutely not!" Silvia turned to Greg. "The only part of a student this man could inspire . . . doesn't need any further stimulation."

Greg let out a laugh, then stiffened his expression.

Fletcher folded his arms and leaned against the doorframe. "Care to make a little bet on it, lady? Give me your most impossible student and in a week I'll have him showing a . . ." He lifted one eyebrow and grinned, "a renascent interest in a higher education."

"Renascent? 'A new life for learning?' I doubt it. In a week, Mr. Sims, the paradigmatic behavior of the student will be ultra vires, and if you don't know what that means, it's that Mister's childish behavior will have advanced beyond any help."

"I have the feeling that I'm missing something here," Greg Evans observed in smothered amusement. "No. I don't think I want to know." He shook his head at Fletcher and Silvia, who both turned to explain. "I think I'll leave you two to work this out. Just keep me posted, will you?"

"Fine," Fletcher agreed. "And thanks for the invitation to the president's tea. Silvia and I will be there with bells— No, make that with gloves on."

"Silvia and I?" Silvia stood, walked around her desk and closed the door behind Fletcher Sims, who had managed to work himself into the room. "Gloves? I assume you mean boxing gloves, because that's what you're going to need. Did we, or did we not, settle this problem you have about answering for me?"

"Oh, this wasn't my decision, Silvie. We've just come from President Woody's office. He's the one who paired us off. You're to be my faculty liaison. By the way, I believe ultra vires means to 'go beyond the specific scope of legal power or authority,' not just help. Which desk is mine?"

"You mean that those poor dumb kids are given full scholarships and then they spend four years taking classes in health and basketweaving and never graduate?"

Hallie nodded. "That's the way Jeff explained it, Fletch. He graduated. But he and the team quarterback were the only ones who graduated the last year he played. Some of those kids couldn't even read the play books."

Fletcher and Hallie were sitting at the kitchen table. After a rousing game of chase with Fletcher, Charlie had been bathed and put to bed. Silvia came in, changed clothes, and left for a theater guild meeting, leaving Hallie on her own.

After sharing a take-out box of Posse's Barbecue, Fletcher had turned the conversation toward growing up in a college town and on the university which had been so much a part of Silvia and Hallie's lives.

"Jeff said that when he was recruited, the school really tried to give minorities every chance. Tutors, special make-up classes, you know the routine. The coaches tried to push them, but unfortunately, for most of them, it was too late. They just weren't prepared."

"And now?"

"At least the high schools try. But now you have drugs and big money to deal with. Still, it's better, I think."

"Yeah, well, looks like your mother and I have our work cut out for us." Glancing around the kitchen, Fletcher gave a contented sigh. Silvia's house was small but warm. Sharing it with Hallie and the boy made a man feel comfortable. Fletcher swung his feet from beneath the table and propped them in the vacant chair next to him.

"Hallie, what happened to your dad?"

"He was killed in a car wreck when I was just a baby."

"I guess it was hard on your mother, raising you alone? Didn't she have any family?"

"No. Grandfather died just before Mother and Dad got married. Mother was young, and scared that she wouldn't measure up. Dad was from an old family and I don't think his parents approved of Mother. They lived in this house. We lived in the apartment until Grandmother and Grandfather died. Mother was a junior then, I think."

"Was it bad, for you, I mean?"

"Bad? No. If it was, I didn't know it. Mother worked hard, going to school, typing term papers, making all our clothes. At least I know now that she did. Back then, it was just Mother, doing what she had to do. She never missed anything I did. And I never told her the things I missed."

"Things you missed?" Fletcher turned back to

face Hallie. The quiver in her voice touched something inside him, some long-forgotten memory of missed birthday parties, missed valentines, and longed-for bicycles and skateboards.

"Oh, there were things I wanted that we couldn't afford. So I didn't tell her. There were places I wanted to go—camp, vacations. But there was no money and no point in both of us feeling bad. Besides, they didn't really matter."

But they had. Fletcher knew. He'd missed them, too, though not for the same reason. Hard work and virtue were the qualities he'd been taught to strive for. And the teaching had come from a virtuous, puritanical woman who enforced those characteristics with a leather strap and a dark closet. And they did matter.

"You got married when you were seventeen?" Fletcher's question wasn't one of condemnation and Hallie knew it.

"Yes. Eloped. Foolish, wasn't I? I was a senior when I met Jeff. It wasn't just that he was a star, he was kind and strong, knew exactly what he wanted in life. We fell in love. He was graduating. I thought that if I let him go to California without me, I'd lose him forever."

"Have you?"

"I don't know. I still love him and I think he loves me. But I can't live in California. I don't want Charlie to be brought up in a place like that. I can't sit back and watch Jeff killing himself. The things they force themselves to do, not just the players, but their wives, too. It's crazy. I don't understand those people and I never will."

"I know what you mean. I've met a few of them. It isn't just California."

There was a long silence. "That's not all of it," she confessed. "I guess we married too young. I was my mother's child, then Jeff's wife. But I don't know who *I* am."

"What about Charlie?"

Her face broke into a smile. "Charlie? He's the most perfect thing in my life. I'm going back to school and get my degree so that I can give him a stable home like I had."

Silvia, outside the door listening, felt a peculiar sensation wash over her. She dropped down on the top step in dismay. Hallie hadn't wanted to discuss her plans and Silvia hadn't forced the issue. She'd thought if she waited, Hallie would explain. Forcing a confrontation was something Silvia couldn't—wouldn't—do.

But Hallie providing the same kind of life for Charlie that she'd had? No, until Silvia had heard Kris Killian's lonely confession of his need for a soulmate, Silvia hadn't begun to understand what her choices had cost her. She didn't want to imagine what it would cost Hallie.

Silvia didn't know how long she'd been sitting there when she heard the chair legs scrape, indicating that Hallie and Fletcher were finished. Swallowing a lump in her throat, she stood hurriedly and opened the screen door just as Fletcher Sims stepped out on to the porch.

"Evening, Silvia. Did you have a good meeting?"

"Er, yes, thanks."

He waited, looking at her as if he expected some further comment. "Well then, good night." His voice dropped, and he paused for a long minute before adding softly, "Nani momi."

"Yes. Good night." She brushed past, leaving him standing on the porch in the darkness.

The kitchen was empty, and the door to Hallie's room was closed when she went up stairs. Silvia felt an odd detachment as she removed her clothes and put them away. Hallie's disclosure had disturbed her. She felt a sense of failure that she hadn't asked her child specifically what was wrong when she came home.

What was even more worrisome was that Hallie had confessed her troubles to a stranger, not her mother. She hadn't wanted emotional confrontations, but she hadn't wanted to be closed out, either. Fletcher Sims had managed to entangle himself in the innermost parts of their lives and Silvia didn't know how to stop his intrusion.

"Nani momi." His words ran through her mind over and over. Nightwing words, no doubt, for they weren't in her dictionary. He'd stumped her, and like the intermittent melody of a forgotten song, the words drifted round and round in her mind as she tried to sleep.

Where was Fletcher Sims's pesky Nightwing when she needed answers? Where was someone to comfort and hold her when she was alone? Why was Fletcher Sims constantly on her mind?

Across the yard he was probably sleeping like some drunken sailor on leave. He couldn't have any idea of the havoc his presence was causing.

She thought she'd never let anybody invade her privacy as he was doing. In spite of every effort to avoid him, everywhere she turned she ran into Fletcher Sims—in her home, in her small office, and in her classes.

Despite her doubts she'd hoped that his presence might add some classroom stimulant. But after three days neither she nor Fletcher had made any appreciable impression on Mister Raschad, though the other students seemed to be making some effort to learn. After three days of sharing her office she was ready to scream from frustration.

One minute it was "What do you think of Underground Atlanta, Silvia?"

"I don't know. I haven't been there."

The next, he would ask casually, "Did you read about the new Sports Medicine and Rehabilitation Center they've built just outside of Augusta in Monticello?"

"No," she'd admitted. "I don't keep up much with sports. I leave it to the kids."

"Uh huh, don't forget that we're going with Kris to see the Dawgs play football. I for one intend to be a loyal Bulldogs fan."

Everyday it was something else. The man was like a chameleon, except the color and flavor Fletcher took on was that of the community, the campus, her world. In less than a month he seemed more at home here than she did. And one way or another, he insisted on involving her in whatever he learned.

He hadn't kissed her again.

But every time he came close to her, he found

a way to touch her. Her body felt as if it were skidding around beneath her skin like mercury from a broken thermometer. She shivered and closed her eyes. She wouldn't look across at the garage. She wouldn't open her window. There weren't any wings brushing against her windowpane. The whispering sound she heard was only a tree limb grazing the house.

Oh, lordy. What on earth was she going to do?

"Charlie go, too, Fwesh!"

"Not this time, sport." Fletcher knelt and spoke directly to the boy. "This time I'm taking your grandmother. But you and I will go to the park and we'll practice throwing the football like your daddy, OK?"

From inside the house Silvia watched Charlie shake his head stubbornly, then reluctantly nod his agreement. There was no question about it, Fletcher had a way of talking to children that made them equals. They respected him and followed his directions—everybody except Mister Raschad.

Mister, the reason she'd finally agreed to go to the football game, was standing beside Kris Killian, who was leaning against a van with the insignia Killian Ranch embossed on the side. Silvia took one final glance at herself in the mirror and went downstairs and into the yard. Looking at herself in one of Hallie's outfits made her more nervous than she already was.

"Silvia!" Fletcher's surprise slipped out.

"Wow, Ms. Fitzpatrick, you look neat. You sure you want me along, ma'am?" Mister added.

"Go and meet Honey, Charlie," Fletcher instructed. "She's making banana pudding for dessert." He watched the boy run across the yard, cut through the hedge, and dash up the steps into Honey's house. The sight of this Silvia rattled him, and he struggled to collect his composure. Except for the silver bathing suit she'd worn at Kris Killian's ranch, he'd never seen her when she wasn't dressed as a no-nonsense professional.

The woman he was looking at was wearing a red-and-black ankle-length print skirt and a silky black blouse with a matching red sash tied around her waist. Beneath her long skirt, she was wearing soft suede boots that made an accordion ripple at her slim ankles. But the most amazing addition were the long silver earrings that touched her shoulders and the matching chains that jangled around her neck.

Silvia Fitzpatrick was stunning.

Silvia Fitzpatrick smiled hesitantly.

Fletcher Sims nodded his head and held out his hand.

But it was Mister who said it all.

"My mama's gonna love telling everybody in Buttermilk Bottom about this. Me, Mister Raschad, sitting in Kris Killian's seats at Sanford Stadium with Spider Malone and his fox. Man, oh, man, that's fly, really fly. You know what I mean?"

On the way to the game, Mister bridged any awkwardness with a steady stream of sports talk. Kris had arranged for the driver to let them off at the gate nearest their seats on the fifty-yard line.

Inside the Sanford Stadium normal conversation was impossible. They'd just reached their seats when the crowd stood and began to roar.

The cheerleaders had come onto the field and made a tunnel for the players to sprint through. Uga, the white bulldog who was the team's mascot, took his accustomed place. The Red and Black band played "Glory, Glory to Old Georgia," and the fans exploded into a frenzy as the football team ran across the field.

Silvia looked around. She hadn't been to a football game in twenty years, not since she and John had sat on the bridge and watched from the end zone outside the stadium. They'd been wildly in love and ready to face the world. What they hadn't been able to face was a baby and paying bills.

The hill was gone now, replaced by more bleachers filled with more cheering fans, and she was sitting in a seat on the fifty-yard line with two world legends. She felt seventeen again, allowing herself to be swept up in the excitement.

Fletcher caught her hand and smiled. "You look like a student, Silvie."

She squeezed his hand. "Not quite, but I feel like one."

The whistle blew. The kicker kicked the ball and the game began. She liked the way Fletcher tucked his head, bringing it close, his lips almost touching her cheek as he explained what was happening. Their shoulders touched. Their thighs touched. He draped his arm around her, squeezing her arm in excitement when the team made a good move and comforting her when they didn't. Touching was natural in the crowd and she found herself responding by touching him, too. There was an excitement in sharing the emotional intensity of the fans and she let herself go, experiencing a freedom she'd always kept in firm control.

"Look at that move, man!" Mister, perched at the edge of his seat, turned in wide-eyed awe from Kris to Fletcher, and back again. "Mo Willis, he's a bro. Went to South Fulton two years ago. Coach said he'd make it as a wide-receiver."

"Coach was right. But he very nearly didn't," Silvia commented."

"What do you mean, lady? He's got moves that Deion Sanders could use. Nothing wrong with Mo Willis, lady."

Fletch turned his eyes to Mister and spoke slowly but with resolution. "I think, kid, that it's time for you to show a little respect. Your teacher has a name. She's Mrs. Fitzpatrick, and if it weren't for her, you wouldn't be here in Kris's box and your buddy out there wouldn't be playing for the Dawgs."

Mister jerked his attention from the play and turned his suspicious gaze toward Fletcher Sims. "What do you mean, man? Mo Willis is the best receiver in the South. Made All-State. Set a record for catching the ball that nobody's gonna break."

"True," Kris Killian agreed. "Everybody's read about Mo's football record. There's just one problem. He very nearly got kicked out of school before he ever made the team."

"Why? Mo don't do drugs and he don't fool

around. You don't know what you're talkin' about."

"He knows," Fletcher said dispassionately. "Your friend Mo was a fake. He had a great memory. He could memorize the playbooks in high school. But he couldn't fool the freshman coach and he couldn't make it in class. Because Mo Willis had a big secret. Mo couldn't read."

Mister jerked his head around, focusing his attention on the action. Only Silvia saw him swallow hard and curl his fingers into a tight fist.

"He was in one of my classes, Mister," she explained. "But he refused to let me help him. Nobody knew his secret, and he was afraid that he'd be laughed at if he told the truth."

"That ain't so," Mister argued. "He got a diploma. He could read as good as anybody.

"No," Silvia corrected. "Your friend couldn't read."

"Naw! He couldn't have fooled everybody like that."

Fletcher could see that the plan wasn't working. Mister was refusing to accept the truth. He'd have to do it, the thing he'd promised he'd never do. "Why not?" Fletcher asked, "it's possible to fool people into believing that you can read when you can't. I know. *I* did."

"What're you saying, man? You jiving me. You're a writer. How can you write them words if you can't read?"

Silvia held her own breath. She knew what Fletcher was doing, but lying to the boy wouldn't work. Inspiration could only go so far. Still, as she looked at Fletcher's face she saw something she had only seen a hint of before. He'd dropped his guard completely. No quick quips, no brash smooth talk. He wasn't lying. The man was telling the truth.

"I had to learn about being honest, Mister. But it took me a long time and a lot of failures before I admitted the truth and accepted help."

"You? Ah, come on, Fletch. *You* couldn't read?"

"I had a problem. I didn't know what it was then. Now they have a name for it, dyslexia. It meant that you see letters different from everybody else. For a long time even my mother thought I was stupid. I thought so, too."

"Having dyslexia doesn't make you stupid, Fletcher," Silvia said softly. "Surely you know that now."

"Sure. Now I do. But try telling that to a twelve-year-old kid whose mother is screaming at him, holding a bel—" His voice trailed off, and he swallowed the word belt. "I think I'll get us a hamburger." He stood up, turned, and fled up the steps.

Fletcher had known that this wasn't a good idea. Coming to the campus had only opened up old wounds, that old sense of failure that had been conquered. . . . But still it lingered, like an invisible finger pointing at him. He never should have allowed Greg to talk him into joining his teaching staff.

But Greg had been certain that Fletcher could relate to the slow learners, that he'd be an inspiration. Greg understood better than most the problems a slow student encountered, for he'd been the one to teach Fletcher how to read.

When Greg first contacted Fletcher's agent with his idea, Fletcher had refused. Nobody knew his secret. Nobody knew that Fletcher Sims, best-selling fiction writer, had once been labeled retarded and punished for not applying himself. But Greg had insisted. When he'd finally agreed, Fletcher told himself it was his way of repaying the debt he owed Greg. He honestly thought he'd put the pain behind him long ago. But he'd been wrong.

After Fletcher left, Silvia looked at Kris with regret in her eyes. "I didn't know, Kris," she said.

"How could you? We all have our secret failures. I can understand how he feels. I told you I ran away from home. What I didn't tell you was that I flunked out of school first."

"Ah, not you, too." This time Mister didn't argue. Too much in awe of the men he was with, he dropped his own tough-guy attitude and listened.

"Oh, it wasn't that I couldn't read. I could. I just got in with the wrong crowd, did drugs, you know the routine. I had to get all the way to the bottom before I learned. Wasted a lot of years, I did. And even then I was lucky or I'd have been dead."

"Man, I'm not believing this," Mister argued. "You made it big. You're Kris Killian and he's Spider Malone. You telling me that I can do it, too? No way. I'm just a dummy from Buttermilk

Bottom. Even if I wanted to, I could never learn all that stuff in time."

"Yes, you can," Silvia disagreed. "Fletcher and Kris learned, but only because they got smart and let someone help them learn. Which is what I'm here for. What do you say? Be honest with the class. If you give it a try, everybody else will follow you."

"It isn't too early to learn to be a leader, Mister," Kris said. "The man who can influence others is the one who captains the team, leads the band, or writes the books."

The stadium suddenly exploded as everyone stood in a riot of cheering. Mo Willis had taken a punt and run it all the way for the first touchdown of the day. During the ensuing hurrah Fletcher returned with the food, and nothing more was said about learning while they ate.

To Silvia, Fletcher's revelation had been a bombshell. He didn't have to say the word "belt" for her to complete his sentence. She couldn't imagine the kind of woman who would whip a child she considered retarded. She couldn't imagine ever thinking Fletcher was slow. He was too quick, too vital, too alive. Everything about the man challenged and stimulated everyone he came in contact with. It seemed that with every direction she turned, a new side to Fletcher Sims was revealed. But this confession put a strain on the day.

Any touching between them now was accidental. The moment of closeness was gone and she didn't know how to recapture it. In the bright warm fall sunshine, Silvia shivered and instinctively leaned against Fletcher's shoulder.

She felt him stiffen for a moment, then as the field goal kicker made the extra point, the fans stood again. As the score flashed on the boards, the roar of the crowd swept through the stands like a freight train. Grown men jumped up and down and hugged each other. It seemed only natural to move into Fletcher's arms. They didn't speak. They wouldn't have known what to say.

FIVE

Their relationship had changed. Silvia knew it from the moment they stepped out of Kris Killian's car. She'd been the first to alter it. By wearing Hallie's dress, she'd announced that she was different. Then Fletcher had revealed his painful past. Neither was the person they had been but they didn't know yet who they'd become.

The house was silent. Silvia was glad that Hallie was still out, for when Fletcher closed the door behind them and pulled her into his arms, she went willingly.

His kiss was rough, passionate, demanding, searing her with the wrenching admission of his need. She needed to understand. But her need was submerged by his taste and touch. Answers were suddenly unimportant. The words they'd bandied about had turned into powerful feelings and there was no putting voice to the wonder of her response.

"Why me?"

They both broke away, gasped, and uttered the same breathless question.

Then swallowed it as their lips found the only answer they needed.

Then she pulled back. "Are you hungry?" she asked abruptly, looking up at him.

Fletcher slowly slid his hand to her neck, cradling her head gently, hoping that he could regain control of his feelings. "Oh, yes, Silvia. I'm hungry. But I think we both know that it isn't for food."

Silvia took a quick breath and swallowed hard, trying to find the strength to deny that she understood his words.

"I know this sounds foolish, but I don't know how to talk about . . . about—this, Fletcher. I'm truly flattered. I never expected a man like you to be interested in me. I understand desire. To you, sex is as normal as eating or sleeping. But it isn't so simple for me."

He took her face in his hands, and with eyes as turbulent as the ocean in a storm, he studied her. "You're wrong, Silvia. I haven't been with a woman in months. I haven't wanted to—until now. What I want is for you to tell me what you feel, deep inside. Tell me your truth, Silvia Fitzpatrick."

Silvia felt as though she were caught in some kind of bright light, being forced to bare her innermost thoughts. Fletcher had shared himself with her, drawing her to him in honest need. What was *her* truth? Why was he forcing her to search for reasons when all she wanted to do was feel his arms around her again. What had happened to her control?

"I'm afraid," she finally murmured.

"So am I, darling. You scare the hell out of me." His words were wrenched from some inner place that channeled his anguish through fingertips that dug painfully into her skin. "Ahhhh, Silvie," he groaned, "who cares about truth."

Then she was back in his arms, being crushed in his desperate embrace. For a long time he held her, not kissing, not moving, not talking—just allowing the intensity of his touch to express his agony.

They heard the slam of a car door and Hallie's voice outside. Fletcher loosened his grip and stepped away, glancing down at Silvia with a long look of disappointment.

"Clichéd interruption, darling. End of love scene. The protagonists are caught in an embarrassing situation by the contrived appearance of the heroine's daughter. My editor wouldn't allow this in a thousand years."

"Real life!" Silvia laughed weakly, as she turned to the sink. "You can't write a novel to compare with it."

Hallie opened the screen door, lowered Charlie down from his position on her hip and called out, "Mother? Are you home?"

"In here, Hallie. Fletcher and I are making coffee."

Hallie walked into the kitchen and took a long look at what Silvia knew must be a flush on her face. She could see her mussed hair in her reflection in the window. She tried to speak, to explain away the intensity of the feelings still washing around the room, but her words failed her.

"Well, well, what have we here? An indiscreet moment in the making, or have we been riding more motorcycles?"

"Of course not, Hallie," Silvia snapped, jerking the coffeepot from its maker and filling it with water.

"Too bad," Hallie said brightly and walked on through. "I'd say a little indiscretion might be just what you need, Mother. Come along, Charlie. Time for a bath and bed."

"Hi, Gran, Fwesh. Charlie sleep Mommy's bed?" Charlie whined, turning sleepy eyes dolefully on his mother.

Hallie looked from her mother to Fletcher Sims and back again. Then she grinned. "Why not, Charlie. Every woman needs a man in her bed now and then. I'll even read you a fairy tale—about a charming prince who awakened Sleeping Beauty with a kiss."

"Hallie!" This time it was Fletcher's voice that was filled with censure.

Hallie stepped in the hallway and turned back around. "I'm sorry, Mother. That was—tacky. I don't know what made me say that. You and Fletch, it's OK with me. I guess I'm just jealous."

"Hallie . . ." Silvia began, "it isn't what you think. I mean . . ."

"Yes, it is, Hallie, but it shouldn't be." Fletcher whirled around and left the kitchen, slamming the door behind him. "I'll pick you up after lunch tomorrow, Silvia—for the president's tea."

"No. I don't think so," Silvia managed to call after him. "I think you should go with Greg Evans."

Fletcher stopped. "I probably should, but we both know I'm not going to. Hey, Honey?" he yelled out. "Got any coffee on the stove? Spider Malone is headed your way."

The next day after church, Silvia, Hallie, and Charlie had lunch at Morrison's Cafeteria. On the way home Silvia stopped by the market for milk and bread. At the same shopping center she picked up a box of ribbons for her printer, and agreed to let Charlie choose a new toy. After testing every item on the shelf he finally settled on a football so that he could practice with "Fwesh" before his daddy came.

Hallie winced at his reason.

Silvia glanced at her watch.

"It's nearly three o'clock, Mother. Don't you think we've killed enough time?" Hallie asked casually.

"I don't know what you mean."

"Sure you do. You and Fletcher are supposed to go to the president's tea together, aren't you?"

"So I was told. But I've never gone to one of those things with—anyone. It's bad enough that I have to share an office and the classroon with him. Everybody there will get the wrong impression. They'll gossip."

"Of course they will. Every woman there will

envy you. Enjoy it, Mother. Besides, I thought this was practically a command performance."

Silvia didn't answer. Charlie began to whine. He was tired and needed a nap. Hallie was right. It was time they went home. She'd figure out some excuse for missing the tea.

But Fletcher Sims hadn't gone without her. He was sitting at the kitchen table casually reading the Sunday paper. He looked up.

"Somehow I didn't think you were the kind of woman who liked to make an entrance," he said. "But I'm willing if you are."

He stood. She wished he hadn't.

Fletcher Sims in a feathered mask was a mysterious attraction. In hip-hugging jeans and a baseball cap he was a wicked, bad-boy centerfold. But in a suit, he was quite simply the most handsome man she'd ever seen.

"Look, Fwesh," Charlie darted in and tugged at his trouser leg. "Charlie's football. Go to the park now and throw?"

"Not today, sport. Tomorrow. Right now your grandmother and I are going to have tea."

"And you, young man, are going to take off your Sunday-school clothes and have a nice nap while your mother studies." Hallie took Charlie's hand and together they climbed the stairs.

"You don't really think I'd go without you, did you, Silvia?"

"No, but I hoped."

"Why? Are you that afraid of me?"

"No. I'm afraid that someone saw us at the game. Suppose they say something? They'll know."

"Know what?"

"That you've kissed me. That you had your hands all over me."

"Wait a minute. Do I have a scarlet 'L' for lover branded on my forehead? So what if they saw us at the game? We weren't doing anything that half the people in the stadium weren't doing. And I haven't had my hands all over you—not yet."

"There you go again, talking like Spider Malone. What if somebody heard you?"

"There's nobody here but Hallie, and somehow I don't think she'd be surprised. Now go powder your nose, or whatever women do, and we'll leave. On the way I have a surprise for you."

"What?" Silvia was suspicious. So far she'd made Fletcher Sims a token partner in her business, ridden a motorcycle, attended a college football game for the first time in twenty years, and been kissed by a legend. She didn't know whether or not she could survive any more surprises.

"I think that this is something you're going to be very pleased to hear. Go get ready."

"We'll take my car, right?"

"Right. I'll even let you drive."

The quick, sweet kiss he planted on her forehead sent her scurrying to comply, as he'd known it would.

Silvia quickly pulled the brush through her hair, leaning close to the mirror as she examined her face curiously. Her skin was glowing, her dark eyes lit with a special light that even she couldn't miss. She felt like a firecracker, her fuse lit and smoldering, ready to explode.

"I know how you feel." Hallie's voice came from behind her.

Silvia jerked back, dropped the hairbrush, and picked up a lipstick. She tried to apply it, felt the tip slide past her lip, smearing awkwardly. Dropping the case, she leaned against the dressing table and closed her eyes.

"I don't know what you mean, Hallie."

"Oh, yes you do. You're like a can of cola being shaken, bottling up all that fizz inside—and sooner or later you'll explode. Believe me, I understand."

"How could you?" Silvia took a deep breath. What was she doing, talking with her own child about feelings that she couldn't, shouldn't, admit to. This was private. This was frightening. This was overwhelming.

"Because. I talked to Jeff yesterday. He called while you were at the game."

Silvia turned around, her own anxiety forgotten in her concern for Hallie. "You did?"

"Yes. Just the sound of his voice made me crazy. Oh, yes. I know how you feel and it's not going to get any better."

"What did Jeff want?" Silvia didn't know whether the question she asked was any safer than the one she wanted to. She didn't know how a woman kept herself from feeling that way and she couldn't ask. As a mother she couldn't discuss her feelings with her daughter. Hallie might be able to talk about desire, but Silvia couldn't. There were seventeen years between them, but today, it felt more like fifty.

"His team will be playing the Falcons in Atlanta in three weeks. He wants me to come over for the weekend."

"Are you going?"

"I haven't made up my mind yet. What about you?"

"I don't understand what you mean." Calmly, Silvia scrubbed the color from her lips and reapplied it.

"You and Fletcher Sims. He's interested in you, Mother. I think you ought to go for it. A man like that is hard to find. Stop hiding your head in the sand. You may regret it if you lose him."

"Silvia?" Fletcher called up the stairs. "You'd better hurry. If I get fired, I can't pay my rent."

"I'm coming." Silvia recapped the lipstick, gave a final pat to her hair, and hurried past her daughter, closing her eyes to Hallie's knowing smile.

At the top of the steps, she stopped. "You know, Hallie. I haven't tried to interfere in your life, but maybe I should have. I think that you ought to take your own advice. If you love Jeff, don't lose him."

Wisely, Fletcher didn't comment on Silvia's worried expression as she drove across campus to the president's mansion. No flowing skirts and dangling earrings this afternoon. Gone was the Gypsy look of the lady who'd cheered wildly at the ball game. Today she was Associate Professor

Silvia Fitzpatrick. Considering his volatile state of mind, maybe that was best.

Still, he liked the dark-red dress she was wearing. It was elegant. The fabric swished as she moved. He liked the serious way she considered whatever was bothering her. Her lips moved as if she where silently arguing with herself, about him most likely. He liked the shape of her ears and the tiny pearls she'd threaded through them. Idly he wondered what she'd do if he slid across the seat and nibbled at that lobe. Sooner or later they were going to get past the necking stage to making real love.

That thought sobered him, bringing a frown to his own face. Real love. He wasn't sure exactly what those words meant. Had his father and mother ever made real love? They'd had him, so they'd slept together at some point in their lives, though by the time he was old enough to be aware, they had separate rooms.

His father had been gone so much that he seemed never to live there at all and then he'd died, far away in Korea, in a "foolish war," according to his mother, that accomplished nothing. Unable to deal with an absent husband and a rebellious son, his mother had found other ways to fill her life—nightly prayer meetings and study groups, seeking perfection in an imperfect world. Finally, Fletcher fled from the punishment inflicted in the name of love.

He considered himself a man when, at sixteen, he'd met Greg Evans, a young college student who volunteered his time to help the disadvantaged.

The night school where Fletcher had been sent was Greg's first assignment. A more unlikely pair had never become friends. And in the end, Greg Evans had taught a street kid that he was neither stupid nor retarded.

By the time Fletcher followed in his father's footsteps and went off to the other side of the world to participate in another insignificant foolish little Asian war, his mother was dead, and Fletcher never went back home. Little wars eventually turned into little stories bought by magazines read by other ex-fighters and misfits. The little stories turned into books and Fletcher Sims never stopped moving again.

Silvia guided the automobile into a side street and found a spot a short distance from the president's house. She cut the engine and picked up her purse. She'd managed not to think consciously about the man sitting beside her. But she wouldn't be able to do that once they were inside.

"Well, darling, shall we peregrinate the drive and be desipient guests at this bodacious affair?"

She knew that he was trying to put her at ease by challenging her mind, but a return quip wasn't forthcoming. "If you mean go inside, I suppose we don't have a choice. But if I'm to be responsible for you, I'd sincerely appreciate it if you wouldn't play Spider Malone and do something foolish."

Fletcher got out of the car and met Silvia at the sidewalk in time to close her door. He tucked her arm beneath his and started up the drive, bending his head as he said, "Believe me, darling, Spider Malone would never embarrass his lady."

Silvia jerked her arm away and hastened up the sidewalk to the porch. Before climbing the steps she turned back to Fletcher, and in her best school teacher voice announced, "I'm not your lady, Fletcher Sims, or Spider Malone, or whoever you are. How many times do I have to tell you that?"

"Till we both believe it, darling. Shall we go in?"

Silvia was saved an answer by the door opening and Greg Evans hurrying out.

"Hurry, hurry. You two are very late."

Greg was a dear, but there were times when he reminded Silvia of the Mad Hatter in *Alice in Wonderland*. All he needed to do was pull out his pocket watch and scurry down a rabbit hole. But it wasn't a hole, it was a door he went through. And it wasn't the Red Queen, but a good portion of the faculty that looked up curiously as they followed Greg inside.

For a time, Fletcher Sims stayed at Silvia's elbow. He was pleasant and seemed genuinely interested in the other staff members. Any self-consciousness she felt quickly dissolved in a kind of comfortable haze. She hadn't realized how nice it was to be with someone. Fletcher Sims, like his counterpart, Spider Malone, seemed completely at home with the faculty. She sensed that Fletcher would fit in just about anywhere he wanted to go.

One of the coaches borrowed Fletcher to discuss his thoughts of motivating some of their players, leaving Silvia behind and furious. After all, she shared the same students and dealt with the same problems as Fletcher Sims. The good old boy network was still very much alive, even if they went to great lengths to pay lip service to the equality of women in the athletic department.

For a time she wandered aimlessly around until she realized two things; first that her feelings weren't the issue here—finding ways to motivate students was. And if having a writer like Fletcher Malone made a difference, she'd be the first to make use of him. Second, the conversations she was taking part in carried a decidedly frosty air.

Silvia shouldn't have been surprised. After all, the world of academia was well known for its snobbish, moral attitude. She should know, she'd been made aware of their point of view years ago when she'd first worked with students at her home after hours. Only when she bought a license and gave her business, Options, Inc., a name was she allowed to work without gossip. Except for Greg Evans, the younger, more liberal professors were still in the minority, and nobody knew that better than Silvia.

The faculty didn't need to have been at the game yesterday to lift lofty eyebrows at her for arriving with Fletcher. His living in her apartment was enough.

From across the room, Fletcher watched Silvia. She was an enigma to him. She didn't pursue him, didn't appear to be in awe of him either as a writer or a man. There was an inner gracefulness about her that promised calm. Finally it came to him. She was like an oasis in the wilderness, providing nourishment, gentleness, and comfort without demanding anything from anyone she gave sustenance to. Silvia Fitzpatrick was the kind of woman men went to war for and came home to after the battle was won.

He'd watched her work in her office, seriously, with quiet determination, choosing and discarding until she'd come up with a brochure with which Kris Killian would be pleased. At school, in spite of their feigned disinterest, she'd quickly become both proud mother and disciplinarian to her students. And she did it without force or criticism. It was because of Silvia that Mister had called a special study meeting this morning. They all wanted to make her proud.

As the coaches' conversation drifted from grades to the next game, Fletcher wandered over to where Greg was standing.

"You like her, don't you, Fletch?"

Greg Evans's inquiry was casual, but Fletcher sensed a proprietary interest in his question.

"Yep. She's a unique woman."

"She's more than that, Fletcher. She's special. The remedial students need her, but that kind of work burns a teacher out, particularly a perfectionist like Silvia. And, frankly, I worry. I'd hoped you might make her relax."

"She's good," Fletcher admitted. "I never had anybody like her as a teacher when I was a kid. If I had, who knows how I might have turned out."

"You'd still have been an outlaw, friend."

"Why does she do it? Her business seems to be a success. And I know she's good at that, too."

"I think that when Hallie eloped, Silvia considered herself a failure as a parent. Afterward she made her students her family. She keeps giving herself away in little pieces and she doesn't even know she's doing it. I wouldn't want to see her hurt.

"Yeah, I see what you mean. Still, this kind of commitment must be hard emotionally. One way or another she keeps losing them over and over again."

"Just remember, Fletcher, she isn't a love 'em and leave 'em woman. She knows the students aren't really hers, so she sets boundaries. You're a different kind of danger to her. I don't know how she'd handle losing you. It took her a long time to get over John's death."

At least she had somebody to get over, Fletcher thought as Greg wandered off to circulate. Greg was right about one thing—Silvia was a candy-and-flowers, church-on-Sunday kind of woman. And he was a making-love-in-the-moonlight, traveling man. She was the life he'd never had and he was finding it very appealing.

This was not good. Sooner or later, they'd better exchange some normal, honest truths about empty lives and temporary fulfillment. Because temporary was what he was, all he could ever be. The problem was that every time they were alone all he did was kiss her or argue with her.

Across the room, Silvia glanced at her watch. She was surprised to find that they'd been there only an hour. Nobody had said anything directly about Fletcher, at least nothing that would be considered out of the ordinary. But she'd found herself explaining over and over that it was at Greg Evans's request that she'd opened her garage after having left it vacant for years.

All afternoon teachers she barely knew sought her out, beginning by asking her opinion on department policies, then sliding into a comment about Fletcher.

"I understand that he's working with your students. Was that planned?"

"And you're sharing an office? Really?"

"I can't imagine what Greg Evans expects a man who writes that kind of junk to teach. What kind of students are we turning out now?"

On and on it went until Silvia felt like a ventriloquist's dummy complete with painted-on smile, parroting a defense of Fletcher Sims. She'd expected them to raise their literary hackles, to be outraged at the appointment of a hack writer to the artist in residence program, but she hadn't expected the snide innuendoes.

She was standing at the punch bowl when Greg Evans joined her.

"I'm really pleased with the progress you and Fletcher are making with the athletes, Silvia. I knew this was a good idea. Don't you agree?"

"I don't know, Greg. It's too early to tell yet."

"Well, I'd call having your students set up a Sunday-study session on their own a step in the right direction."

"They did what?"

"You mean you don't know?"

"No, I'm afraid I don't."

"I was going to tell you, Silvia," Fletcher said, laying his hand on her shoulder. "On the way over here. But somehow we got off on another subject."

He'd said that he had something to tell her. But Silvia had been so shaken by Hallie's information and the challenge that she'd issued to her daughter that Fletcher's statement had gone right out of her head. This kind of loss of direction was new and disturbing.

"Who called a study session?"

"Mister. Seems our little football outing worked. He gathered up his fellow athletes and came by right after you left for church this morning. We talked things over and they've decided to put in a double shift."

"Good work, Fletcher. I'll find you an empty classroom. I knew you were the right man for the job. You and Silvia make a good team."

Fletcher put down his empty cup. "Think so? So do I."

Silvia started to disagree, but Greg had already slipped away and Fletcher was staring at her. He didn't have to say the words, *I want you,* his eyes did it for him.

Silvia felt her knees turn to vanilla pudding. She looked at him and let out a long breath. "You've had too much punch to drink, Spider Man. It's overstimulated your brain."

"It isn't my brain that's overstimulated, lady."

"Yes. That, too." Once again her nerve endings were curling like quivery little jellyfish just under her skin. Simply being near him turned into a painful longing that she didn't seem to be able to stop.

She'd been alone too long. She'd had years to perfect her defenses against every conceivable assault. But she had no defense against loneliness. Even Hallie's return hadn't changed that because she'd known it was only temporary. Fletcher Sims had put on that funny pair of wings and flown over her boundaries. And she knew that he was temporary, too.

"Why, Fletcher? Why do you keep coming on to me? I'm not your kind of woman."

"Let's get out of here and talk, Silvia. We need—"

"You're right," she interrupted. "We need to talk. I don't want a lover, Fletcher. A friend I can talk to, maybe. But I can't talk to you if you keep touching me. Promise me that you'll stop touching me. The faculty is already whispering about us."

Fletcher looked down at his hand. He'd gathered up a bunch of the red material of her dress in his fingers and he was making little circles across the cap of her shoulder like a cat kneading the person he loved. He was surprised that he wasn't purring.

Maybe he was. There was a rhythmic sizzle in his motions. He could hear it even if Silvia couldn't.

"I'll try," he managed weakly as he herded her through the guests and toward the door. "But it seems to me that you already have enough friends.

Maybe we both ought to think about changing our needs."

She saved her question until they were sitting in the car, on the street in front of the president's home, where everyone passing by could see them. Silvia figured they would be safe there. They could talk without Fletcher touching her.

"Changing needs. What does that mean?"

She was wrong about being safe. Fletcher reached out and took her hand, frowning as he considered his answer.

"Silvia, you already have plenty of friends. What you need is a lover. I, on the other hand, haven't had many friends. And I think I might like you to be one."

"That's impossible. If I'm your friend and you're my lover, there's no way to separate the two."

"But we've both been doing it, haven't we? I've been making love to you since the first moment we met. And, whether or not you intended to, you've become my friend."

"Well, yes. I suppose that's correct, but the truth is—it's wrong."

"We're two reasonably intelligent people, Silvia, honest people. If together we can sell Kris Killian's ranch and teach Mister how to read, we ought to be able to solve both our problems—together."

She looked down at his hand holding hers and back to his roguish face.

His voice was low and hesitant. "Please?"

As Silvia watched, the intense look in Fletcher's

eyes melted, turning into little-boy wistfulness. She felt her own resolve begin to weaken. "How?"

"I promised Greg I'd be here ten weeks. I was a week late and a week has already gone. That leaves us eight weeks to go. Why don't we start over. Do nothing for a while as we research the problem, study our motivation. Then we'll each make an outline of the action we think best suited to our . . ." He started to say affair, changing it instead to, "joint venture."

"We're not writing a book here, Fletcher."

"No, we're planning a temporary, meaningful relationship." He leaned forward as if he were about to kiss her, then stopped himself. He swayed back and forth for a moment before he moved away and dropped her hand. "Let's go home, Silvia. We have some serious plotting to do."

"Plotting?" Silvia felt cheated. She hadn't known how much she wanted to be kissed until he didn't do it. Her skin twinged from the withdrawal of his touch. She frowned. His touch kept her constantly aware of him as a man. In spite of her protest. She was beginning to crave that touch. Maybe friendship wasn't the kind of relationship she wanted. Maybe a temporary relationship was better than nothing.

Silvia started the car. A series of quick nervous yawns swept over her. Since Fletcher Sims landed on her back porch she hadn't slept well.

Maybe Hallie was more right than she knew.

Maybe the story they were plotting had already been written.

Maybe Prince Charming had awakened Sleeping

Beauty. Except the world he was awakening her to was frightening. All in all she thought she'd have preferred another fairy tale. Maybe she'd like Fletcher Sims better as a frog.

SIX

For the next three weeks, though it took every ounce of his willpower and tested every facet of Spider Malone's free-wheeling personality, Fletcher Sims kept himself under strict control.

He never intended to extend their hands-off time for so long, but he quickly learned what Silvia had known from the beginning. He hadn't realized that such attitudes still existed, but to some of the faculty members, his very presence in Silvia's garage apartment compromised her status. Anything more than a renter-landlord arrangement would probably make her life impossible after he'd gone.

In the past Fletcher wouldn't have worried about the aftermath of a relationship, certainly not with a woman of thirty-six. But Silvia was different. There was an innocence about her that he wanted to protect.

Fletcher found himself adapting his plan. He was pleasant, affable, friendly. Under the guise of giving them both time to consider what they wanted from each other, he forced himself to stay away for an entire week, then two. He'd never held back from desire before. Now, in spite of the frustration, there was a kind of pride in his restraint.

They shared her tiny office without touching while they talked about their past.

They shared her kitchen without touching while they talked about their dreams.

They taught their classes, working with the students without issuing one challenging word to each other. Even the Nightbird seemed to cooperate.

During the third week, to Fletcher's further amazement their lives seemed to be settling down to a conventional routine, something he'd never thought he could abide. Now he felt great pride in living an ordinary lifestyle, actually looking forward to the familiarity.

Kris Killian sent word that he liked Silvia's proposal, and added only one final suggestion. Members of Mister's special study group passed their first departmental test. Hallie and Jeff talked frequently on the phone.

Fletcher liked the quiet, efficient determination that Silvia applied to whatever she was doing. She'd taken a life left in shambles by the death of her young husband and made a proper home for her child. Never complaining, never blaming others for the blow life had given her, she was a true pioneer woman. She presented a calm, sedate exterior, while Fletcher knew that, inside her private self, she was changing, too. He'd kissed her and felt the promise of her passion. He felt like a child at Christmas, holding a beautifully wrapped package, knowing that inside was some wonderful treasure, yet reluctant to remove the paper. Each day that he held himself back, the anticipation heightened.

The newfound camaraderie of their relationship forced Silvia to admit that Fletcher was kind and gentle. He was infinitely patient with little Charlie. Hallie trusted and confided in him. He'd sparked the students' interest and given Silvia cause to look forward to each day as a new challenge to be shared. She liked having someone to rely on, something she'd missed for too many years. She was beginning to understand that no matter what kind of face Fletcher presented to the world, underneath it all, he was the kind of man any woman would cherish.

Silvia realized that they'd reached some kind of unacknowledged compromise, a no-man's land of undefined but carefully-adhered-to boundaries. Fletcher was in fact becoming a normal man, a man who could be more than a friend, yet was still less than a lover. She hoped that Fletcher was learning that a woman could be less than a lover and perhaps more than a friend.

Fletcher's plan was working. Their lives were completely proper, just what she'd asked for.

So what was wrong?

The spark had become smothered, changing from banked coals to dampened smoke. Silvia was learning to understand another painful truth. In spite of the proper picture they were presenting to the world, life had been more dynamic before they'd decided to admit to, and control, their feelings. When she was still lying to herself about how she felt, every moment had been an exciting challenge.

Now, though they presented an exterior picture of maturity and propriety to the world, inside Silvia Fitzpatrick was disintegrating. They'd taken a sensible path which would allow them to start over and define their relationship. And her emotions were turning into a seething mass of tangled nerve endings and secret longing. In fact, while she enjoyed and related to Fletcher Sims, she truly missed Spider Malone.

Finally, after another night in which she slept badly, Silvia decided that, while she might not be as worldly as Fletcher, the current stalemate had to end. And she had to be the one to end it. What happened now, she'd trust to fate. But she had to find out whether the sparks she and Fletcher set off were enduring or merely a flash fire that would quickly burn itself out from the heat of its passion.

Truth was, she'd decided that the outcome didn't matter. Maybe there were only so many chances offered in a lifetime and it was up to a person to take advantage of them when they came. Maybe she was simply a lonely woman lusting after an exciting traveling man. So what? Hallie was right. She'd be a fool to waste her opportunity. Spider Malone or Fletcher Sims—she wanted him. For tonight, for a month, for however long he stayed.

And if she wanted him, she'd have to be the one to go after him, starting today.

This morning she wouldn't scurry away before Fletcher came over for breakfast. She'd face him. They'd talk privately. She'd convince him that this impasse was killing her. Still in her robe, she kept one ear tuned to the garage, delaying her departure until long after Hallie and Charlie had left for school and the nursery.

But there was no Fletcher. Disappointed, Silvia finally decided that she'd either missed him or that he wasn't coming inside before he left. She dressed and went downstairs.

Fletcher was sitting at the kitchen table, drinking coffee. There were flowers on the table and cold omelets on the stove.

At her entrance he looked up warily.

"I must have overslept. I didn't hear you come in," she lied uneasily.

"I didn't want you to. I couldn't sleep so I got up early and made omelets for us," he offered, his fingers pressed white around the handle of the spoon.

"I thought maybe you'd like to ride in together this morning," she said.

"Thanks. I thought we could have breakfast together," he said.

"I'll reheat the omelets," she said.

"I'll get you some coffee," he said.

Fletcher stood. He nodded his head and turned to pour the coffee while Silvia put the food in the microwave. As they moved toward the counter, their arms brushed. Without acknowledging their reaction, each stepped quickly apart.

But their time for waiting was over. He couldn't stand being apart from her any longer. He was going crazy with wanting her. Yet, changing the status quo was going to be difficult. He'd take it slow, one thing at a time. First, they'd share the breakfast table and a ride.

Next they shared a sandwich for lunch and sat around afterward, talking about safe, inconsequential things, parting only when it was time for Fletcher to meet with his second-session study group.

Midafternoon a dozen pink roses appeared on Silvia's desk. The card said, *from a vertiginous friend.*

Vertiginous? So Fletcher was dizzy and confused. Silvia swallowed hard and smiled. Her man of words was back. He wasn't the only vertiginous one. Her state of mind was pretty dizzy and confused, too.

When Fletcher didn't turn up after class, Silvia threw caution to the winds and went looking for him. She found him, still in the classroom Greg had assigned him, surrounded by an ever-enlarging group of students. He was dividing them into smaller subgroups, instructing them in setting individual goals.

Finding a seat in the rear, she sat down to observe.

After assignments had been handed out for the following day they settled down into a general discussion of life and what they could expect. This was where Fletcher seemed to have the most influence. He tolerated no cop-outs, and no excuses. And the students responded.

"A man is responsible for his own success or failure, his own happiness or unhappiness." He cut through to the heart of the matter and forced the students to do the same.

"Buy why'd you come here, Fletcher? I'd catch the next banana boat and go where the tide took me. Anything's better than working with a bunch of smart a— students like us."

The speaker was a student Silvia didn't know, a thin, sallow-faced girl with bad complexion.

"No, working with you is good. Because you need me. And everybody needs to be needed."

"Need? Tell me about that," the girl went on. "Tell me about having to do the cooking, look after the little ones, be the mama, because your mama is . . . well, let's just say I've had it with that kind of need. I'll take my chances on a banana boat."

"Sure. You could run off and join the French Foreign Legion and live on dried beef and tepid water. And sooner or later you'd find out that you hadn't left trouble behind you. You'd just swapped one kind of problem for another."

"But at least you can start over—fresh," another argued.

"Maybe, but whatever you left behind is still a part of you. You may pretend that you don't care, but you do. And one day, sooner or later, you have to face it. You have to drag out the past and look at it, see how you screwed up, find the truth. Believe me, it's better if you do it before you've wasted half your life feeling guilty about it."

Fletcher wasn't talking to her, but Silvia knew that he might have been. Surrounded by his students, he hadn't seen her come in. She waited until he turned his head and she slipped out of the room. Her heart was pounding and her head felt as if the blood in her veins was filled with air pockets.

How long was she going to keep fooling herself. She'd spent thirteen years trying to hide from the truth, the truth that she'd carried with her from the day John died. She'd been a foolish girl then, fanning a simple quarrel into a full-fledged fight that had carried her young husband out into the night.

If they hadn't been poor. If they hadn't had a baby. If she were better organized, a better cook, had a better job. On and on it had gone, starting with nothing, escalating into something that she didn't know how to stop. And not for the first time. He'd stormed out, frustrated, exhausted, unable to face her recriminations.

The road had been slick. And the car brakes were old. He'd had an accident. But she'd always believed that it had been her fault that he'd had the wreck. And she'd spent the rest of her life trying to make up for being what she'd been—a child bride who didn't know how to manage a baby and a home. She'd blamed herself for John's death and spent the next twelve years punishing herself, twelve wasted years. Was she about to make the same mistake again?

What kind of relationship could she have with a larger-than-life outlaw who lived out every man's greatest fancy in the pages of his books? Was there a chance for any kind of relationship between them? She didn't know. She only knew that he'd forced her to take a long honest look at herself and she wasn't certain she could face the truth. The one thing she did know was that she couldn't close herself off from this man. He wouldn't allow it. And she'd hurt long enough. Perhaps the time had come for forgiveness to begin, forgiveness for herself, for her youth.

Fletcher would soon be gone. Hallie, one way or another, was only back temporarily. How did she want to spend the rest of her life? Time had blurred the edges of her pain. Now Fletcher Sims had forced her to examine her needs with honesty. It was time to face the truth.

Noble words, but if she admitted the truth, what she really wanted was the same thing she'd always wanted, being close to someone, knowing that she was wanted, too. The honest truth was that she wanted Fletcher Sims—for now, for as long as she could hold him. Her tomorrows would be whatever they would be. What she wanted now was to be loved by this man, to make memories that would remain, long after the man she'd made them with was gone.

On Friday afternoon Hallie left for Atlanta and a reunion with her husband. Silvia left Charlie with Honey and drove to the ranch to meet Kris Killian. He viewed Silvia's request with surprise when she voiced it, but he agreed. He accepted her final sales presentation and, before he flew off in his private jet, left instructions with the staff that Silvia and Fletcher would be his guests at the ranch for the weekend.

Now all Silvia had to do was put her plan into action.

As a scene writer she had worked out her motivation.

But as a teacher Silvia knew that her scene was unrealistic, unwise, and contrived. If she were grading her own paper, she'd flunk herself. But this was real life, not fiction. If her plan worked she didn't care what anybody thought, even Honey Watts, who lifted a painted-on eyebrow and smacked her lips when Silvia asked her to baby-sit—for the entire weekend.

Fletcher had been right.

She had enough friends. And she wanted him to be more.

Fletcher had made friends—on the faculty, through his students. The neighbors had taken to him right away. Even little Charlie had adopted him as a stand-in father. Fletcher had found what she'd always thought she needed—friends and family.

Now it was her turn to discover what his idea of their swapping needs really meant. If Fletcher was learning to be a friend, she could learn to be a lover.

Fletcher was in the garage apartment. She'd

watched him drive up on his motorcycle. Tonight she was taking him out to dinner, and though he didn't know it yet, she didn't plan to get home before tomorrow. The chapter was properly outlined in her head. All she needed now was the nerve to implement the action.

Across the yard Fletcher lay on his bed and tried to will time to pass. Charlie was at Honey's. Hallie had driven to Atlanta in her mother's car. Silvia was alone. He tried to erase that picture from his mind. If he expected any relationship with her, he had to go slow, shower her with old-fashioned courting.

His plan wasn't working. His mind imagined that she was taking a shower. It imagined her firm body, the presence of faint little spider marks that said she'd had a child, the full breasts and large nipples of a mature woman. A ripple of intense desire swept over him.

Who was he kidding? He'd come here with the idea of spending a few months of R&R, revving up his creative juices while resting his body. In the last few years he'd gradually run out of steam. A change of scene was supposed to reverse that, but he hadn't counted on a sexy grandmother with keep-off signs posted everywhere he touched.

He hadn't counted on the overwhelming sense of home she'd represented, nor his sudden hunger for a family when he held little Charlie. He'd lived a make-believe life for so long that he'd begun to believe his own tales. The last three weeks had forced him to stand back and examine his feelings.

He cared about Silvia Fitzpatrick. But caring

about somebody might be too honest. Caring made obligations and restrictions.

Honesty forced him to deal with the reality of caring. And no matter how much he denied it, caring meant love, the kind of love that snuck up on a person, and suddenly that person was more interested in making somebody else happy than he was in his own needs.

Fletcher squirmed. Sure, you really are a traveling man, you jerk. You're a fine one to talk about taking care of another person's needs when you're starving from you own. Still, his need wasn't just physical. He and Greg had had a long discussion about sex or the lack of it recently.

"Sex," Fletcher had argued, "is a lot like eating bananas. There was a time, for three months, when I ate bananas three times a day. You know what I learned? No matter how much you like a thing, a straight diet of it will kill your craving."

"How old are you now, Fletcher?" Greg had asked.

"Forty. Too old to be chasing a woman and too young to stop wanting to."

"Maybe," Greg had suggested, "there is a difference between just sex, and sex and love." To Fletcher's surprise he'd confessed that he was considering getting married. Even at his advanced age, there came a time when a man wanted security. "Besides," he'd quipped in embarrassment, "I get tired of talking to the dog. He loves me, but he doesn't keep my feet warm."

It wasn't Fletcher but Spider Malone, who'd

quipped, "Your feet aren't the only thing you want to keep warm, old buddy."

"That, too," Greg admitted sheepishly. "Maybe you ought to consider someone to talk to, too."

"Fine. I'll buy a dog."

But he hadn't been able to stop himself from thinking about Greg's disclosure. Silvia was the kind of woman a man could talk to. She was the kind of woman a man would make love to, too. What had he been thinking of when he'd spouted off about deciding what they wanted from each other?

Wanting Silvia Fitzpatrick physically had surprised him, but he'd wanted women before. Now the wanting was changing, turning into more than just sex. He was moving into uncharted waters here and he wasn't certain that this real-life plot would sell.

What he needed to do was to find out.

What he needed was a hurricane, some kind of natural disaster to force their emotions to the danger level. Danger would bring the relationship to a peak or kill it entirely. Surely as a writer he could conjure up something—but what?

What he got was a knock on his door. Followed by its being opened. Followed by the woman he'd visualized in his bed. Silvia came inside, closed the door, and leaned hesitantly against it.

"Silvia? What are you doing out here?"

She was a different woman this afternoon. Wearing leotards, a ribbed undershirt covered by a long, wide-necked sweatshirt, and the same soft boots she'd worn before, she might have been her daughter. No, Hallie would never be the lush, earthy woman her mother was. She didn't have the life experience.

"Spider Malone's lady has come to take him to dinner."

"She has?" His voice went husky. He sat up. She was having an alarming effect on a body already wired to the breaking point.

"Yes, will he come with me?" She held out her hand.

"Where are you taking him?"

"Does it matter?"

She looked scared, like a little girl at her first piano recital, determined to be brave. He liked the way she waited, her expression softening as he stood, and he placed his large hand in her small, trusting one.

"No."

"We'll take the motorcycle." She was growing more confident now as he stood beside her.

"Whatever you say."

"I say that the lady would like, no, *needs* to be kissed—just once. Then we'll go."

Fletcher lifted her hand, turned it palm up, then lowered his head and softly kissed the center. He felt her grip tighten around his little finger and wished her hands were pressed against his bare skin.

"If Spider Malone kisses you, Silvia, it won't be just once. I don't think we'll ever get out of this room."

"Then Spider's lady will kiss him," she said, planting her lips breathlessly on his. It was meant to be a tease, a quick sample to entice, then she'd move quickly away. But her hands crept up and tangled themselves in his hair. Her tongue slipped inside his mouth, silky, warm, and heady, and her head began to swim.

She forced herself to move away.

"Spider's lady is quite a woman," Fletcher managed to say between the roar of his pulse and the sputtering of his breathing.

"Yes, she is." Sylvia surprised herself with her firm voice. And she was just beginning to understand how much of a woman she was. Silvia stared at Fletcher for a long, uneven moment, then opened the door behind her and led him down the steps into the garage.

Fletcher followed her. Silently he slid their helmets over their heads, snapped the straps in place, and rolled the bike out of the shed into the late afternoon. Every move, every sound seemed sharper, slightly surrealistic. The crackle of the falling leaves beneath their feet, the scrape of the kickstand on the concrete, the sound of Charlie's laughter drifting through the air, Silvia's perfume and her little gasp as she slid into the seat behind him and closed her arms around his chest.

"Where to, lady?"

"We're having dinner at Kris's ranch."

"Kris?"

"He's on his way to California."

"Just Spider and Silvie?"

"Unless he has a luscious nubile or two stashed somewhere I don't know about."

"If he does, I'll drown them." He started the

engine, allowed the machine to roll sedately down the drive to the street. Then, with a wave of his hand to Honey, the machine blasted off, leaving black skid marks on the street and a neighborhood evenly divided between those who cheered with approval and those who chortled with disbelief.

This time Silvia didn't hold back. She leaned against Fletcher, allowing her fingertips to slide beneath his shirt, skipping across his chest. The sun was behind them. Ahead, just over the edge of the horizon, a pale, watery moon hung above the treetops.

Faster, she wanted to cry out. *Tonight I want to fly*.

Like a black winged bird, joined to its mate in flight, they raced through the late-afternoon sunlight. This time it was Silvia who opened the gate.

Inside the atrium, soft music was playing. A table beside the indoor pool was set with flowers and glowing candles. Beside the table was a cart embellished with food in covered silver dishes.

"Are we alone?" Fletcher asked, hearing his voice echo too loud in the large room.

"We're alone."

He walked toward the table, wondering what she expected of him. This uncertainty was new. She'd made a point of calling him Spider, not Fletch. Did she expect Spider to ravish her? He wasn't sure.

"This scene is from your point of view, Silvia. There is no way I can know what you expect to happen. You'll have to let me inside your head."

"I'm afraid that I haven't worked out the details

as well as I thought I had, Fletcher. I just thought that we . . . that you and I . . . I mean that I wanted to,'' she gathered up her courage and willed herself to say it all, ''be with you.''

"Be with me? As in make love?"

"Yes."

"Silvia," Fletcher's voice was soft. "Silvia." He came close. "Are you sure you know what you're saying?"

A shiver of delicious pleasure tumbled through her as Fletcher put his hands on her shoulders. As always, her breath became labored and she couldn't speak. She lifted her lips for the kiss she craved with every part of her. And suddenly she was in his arms, being held close, hearing her name whispered against her hair, her cheek.

Fletcher groaned and found her lips, sliding his fingertips through her hair, down her neck around her slim rib cage until they finally reached her breasts.

Sylvia reveled in his touch, pressing herself against him, meeting his urgency with a delicious heat that flamed up her body like lightning. Her own fingertips were stroking, searching, touching the man who had captured and imprisoned every part of her from the moment their eyes first met.

"Oh, Fletcher," she whispered.

She'd never felt like this before.

Fletcher? It wasn't Spider she was with now. Fletcher's lips slid across her cheek, leaving hot, wet kisses down her neck, branding her flesh with his touch which would be forever imprinted on her body. His lips reached her bare breasts and she hadn't been aware that her clothes were gone. He took her into his mouth, urgently nuzzling, playing, moving in unison with his hands as he explored all her secret, forbidden places. She knew that this was what she wanted, all she ever wanted, and more.

Her low, desperate moan was swallowed up by his lips as he swept her up into his arms and strode across the room into the cabana.

Fletcher knelt, laying her on a satin futon, holding himself over her with his elbows. Her breath was fast and shallow, her great dark eyes veiled and passion-filled as she pressed herself against him. He drew in a deep, heady breath, trying desperately to slow down what was happening.

Silvia hadn't been with a man since her husband had died. She'd told him that. Unbelievable, but he knew that it was the truth. And he was, for the first time in his life, afraid. He hesitated.

"Fletcher? What's wrong?" Her movements slowed and her eyes grew wide.

"Nothing, my darling. I just want to be sure that you understand what you're doing. This isn't Spider Malone and his lady. This is Fletcher Malone and Silvia Fitzpatrick."

"Shush. Do we have to talk, Fletcher? Can't we just feel? Don't you want to make love to me?"

"Oh, yes. I've wanted to make love to you from the first moment I saw you. But I'm not sure how smart this is, for either of us."

Silvia ran her fingers up his chest, pushing the unbuttoned shirt from his shoulders. She raised her head, planting little butterfly kisses across his chest as she found his belt and unbuckled it. Pressing her hand between them she pulled the zipper down, freeing the aching part of him that he couldn't conceal. Now she was touching him, encircling the width and playing up and down its length.

"Oh, lady, what are you doing?"

"I'm spinning my own web."

"You'd better stop that. I've been celibate for too long."

"So have I, Spider Man," she murmured. "And this time, you're in my snare. Make love to me, Fletcher Sims, or I shall surely die."

Her kisses, her wanting him, had set him on fire. There was no turning back. He lifted himself first to his knees where he stripped the remaining clothes from her body, then to his feet, catching the heel of one shoe with his toes and pulling his foot from it. Then the other, before he boldly shoved his jeans and briefs down his legs and jerked himself free.

"God, Silvia, I want you. I've never wanted anybody like this before." He fell across her, felt her open herself to receive him, and before he could force himself to be gentle, he was inside her.

Greedily she took him, matching passion for passion, rising to meet each thrust. Her body, feverish with desire, joined with his in wild abandon until the fire they'd set shattered into glorious release that left both of them stunned in wonder.

For a long time they drifted, still joined,

Fletcher bracing himself on his elbows as he waited for his body to relax and reflect his spent passion. His eyes were closed. Breath after painful breath followed as he tried to regroup his senses. But his newly awakened body refused to have any part of normal downtime before rejuvenation.

Firmly, steadily, it continued to claim the woman beneath him.

Silvia lay, floating in warm nothingness. She'd hoped, imagined, wanted. But what she'd experienced had been beyond the scope of her wildest imagination. Even now, Fletcher throbbed hard inside her.

She opened her eyes slowly, uncertain of what she'd see in his. But his eyes were closed. Never had she seen a man's face after he'd made love. Fletcher was beautiful. There was a hint of a smile tugging at the corners of his lips. His face was slick with perspiration, flushed with satisfaction.

She liked the way her breasts were smashed against his broad, virile chest. The silky dark hair feathered against her skin like millions of tiny jolts of warmth as he breathed. By exhaling at the same time it was as if they were still making love. Only when they both took a deep breath could she see lower, see the place where her dark hair and his met and entwined, see where they were still joined.

And then he was kissing her again. She curled her legs around him and closed her eyes. As they had that first night in the pool, they moved together slowly, tenderly. Fletcher moved his lips away nestling his face behind her ear. He lowered his arms, lowering his body until every part of them was touching before slipping his hands beneath her and catching her buttocks in his hands.

Now he could control their movements, synchronize his entering, pulling back, sliding along her outer lips for long, tantalizing minutes until he plunged back inside again.

Their first coming together was explosive, wild, tumultuous. This time he was content to love her tenderly, waiting for that first tentative flare of desire which he teased almost to a sweet breaking point before coming to a full stop.

Silvia heard her heartbeat. She felt the jerking, unsteady movement of Fletcher inside her as he continued to hold still. Just as she was about to scream, he began to move once more. First kisses, then touching, touching every part of her, then the powerful movement of his body thrusting deep inside her. Over and over again he brought her to the edge, then stopped and let the flame die down again.

This time, when it happened, it was a mutual soaring that began slowly and moved higher and higher until Silvia was certain that they actually were flying through space. Afterward, as they fell back to earth, she felt him slide over to the side and pull her sweetly into his arms. He was whispering to her, indistinguishable words that merged with the feelings and made the moment a forever memory.

It was dark when they finally stirred. The lights of the pool had been turned on and the last colors of the sunset boiled pink above the trees in the distance. Neither spoke. Fletcher simply stood and held out his hand, asking Silvia to follow. Together they walked to the pool and down the steps into the cool silvery water.

Even in the water, they floated together, touching, reveling in the sensation of being close. She leaned against him, reveling in the joy of his strength. He was her anchor, holding her firmly against him while the water lulled them into a state of such relaxation that she almost fell asleep. Finally, they left the pool and pulled on the robes that had miraculously been laid on the backs of the lounge chairs. Fletcher found a towel and rubbed Silvia's hair until it framed her face in lacy wisps.

"Are you hungry, my darling, Silvia?"

"I don't know. All my needs and desires have merged into one glorious sensation. Nothing divides itself out. It's as if my entire body were suspended in silver light. I feel as if I'm floating."

"I know." Together they walked over to the table they'd ignored in what seemed like hours ago. New candles flamed in the darkness. Glasses were filled with shimmering liquid. Their plates lay ready for the food still warm in their containers.

They ate, every flavor a new sensation on their tongues. Every sip of liquid followed by a kiss that moistened and refreshed. From his plate, Fletcher selected food, touched her lips, urging them open with one tasty morsel after another. She accepted what he offered without conscious identification of what she'd eaten.

They talked first of inconsequential things. The

stars, the island, the people Fletcher had known and the places he'd been. Then later, as they tied open the door to the cabana and lay on the futon looking into the night sky, Silvia finally told him about John, the boy she'd fallen in love with when she was sixteen.

She told him of adolescent passions, of frustrated rejections, of longings and desires that neither had been able to control forever. Once she began, Silvia didn't hold anything back.

"We wanted each other, Fletcher," she said, "but we didn't know what to do about it. I wasn't the right kind of girl for him. I was wild, ambitious, anxious to have the kind of life he'd had and I hadn't. My mother was dead. My father was killed in a construction accident and I went to live with my grandfather. There was nobody for me to talk to about what I was feeling, and I was afraid."

"Afraid of letting yourself go?"

Her head was on his arm. Her leg thrown across his bare body. His hand was caressing her breast and she felt as if now, for this moment, there was nothing in the world they couldn't share.

"No, afraid of *not* letting go. You see, I wanted a normal life so much. Maybe if I'd had a mother to talk to, things would have been different."

"Maybe. But John had a mother, didn't he?"

"Yes. John's family was one of the oldest ones in Athens, though they weren't wealthy anymore. But his parents were older and his father had a heart condition. They'd spent most of what they had through the years. They lived in the same house John had been born in. They belonged to a church. They were—normal."

Fletcher gave her a gentle kiss, encouraging her with his touch. "And you thought you weren't?"

"John could have had any girl he wanted. He was already a junior in college. I was a nobody. But I guess I was the only one who ever turned him down. Oh, I don't mean he didn't care about me. He did. He always did. He just didn't have much control."

"At nineteen, darling, none of us did."

"Well, one night we went too far. After that, it seemed foolish to say no. Usually we were careful. But he wanted to make love without—without protection, to experience the sensation. I finally agreed to let him, just . . . I mean he wasn't supposed to."

"But he did and you got pregnant."

"Yes. I could have had an abortion. But I didn't. I couldn't. We got married. That was a mistake."

Fletcher kissed Silvia's forehead. "Darling, Hallie wasn't a mistake."

"No, but it was hard. Much harder than I'd expected. He wanted to graduate. I went to work. You know the story."

"Go on."

"Hallie was born. Then my grandfather died. We'd quarreled about my working so hard. But I had no choice. I didn't know how much I needed him until he was gone. For a long time I thought I was being punished, and I didn't know why. Then John had the car crash and I was sure."

"Oh, Silvia. I'm so sorry. You didn't do anything but care too much. I wish I could take all that pain away. But I can't. I couldn't even take away my own."

Silvia felt the sudden tension in Fletcher's body. She laid her head against his chest, pushing hard as though her body were a sponge, and by pushing she could absorb his anguish. "Tell me about it."

"My father died, too. I'd become something of a rebel. My mother couldn't cope. She turned herself over to her church and turned me out on the street. The family of a buddy of mine took me in for a while. But eventually I hit the road."

"How old were you?"

"I left when I was fourteen. When I was fifteen I got into a little scrape with the law and they put me into a group foster home. That saved my life, that and what they called an alternative night school, where a teacher learned about my reading problems."

"Greg Evans?"

"Yep. Because of Greg I graduated from high school and worked my way through four different colleges before I eventually graduated from a two-bit night school in Texas. You want to hear something really funny? My degree is in education. You want to know something else? Greg Evans saved my life."

Silvia stared up into the darkness, watching the last patch of pink disappear as she thought about what Fletcher had been through. His life had been vastly different from hers, yet really they weren't so different after all.

They'd both cared too much and they'd both found a way to hide their pain.

It was very strange that they'd both met Greg as students, at a time they needed help. He'd taught them both. Maybe he still was.

"Dear, dear Greg," she whispered. "Thank you. I think maybe that you've saved my life, too."

SEVEN

The car was in the garage when Silvia and Fletcher returned. Fletcher killed the motorcycle engine and sat for a long minute without speaking. They were home and he didn't know yet what that meant. Almost reluctantly they both got off the bike and removed their helmets, slowly, making no attempt to pretend that they weren't prolonging the moment.

"Silvia?"

"Yes?"

They moved into each other's arms for one last desperate private moment.

"Silvia, I don't know whether or not I can hide the way I feel about you now, after this."

"You must. I don't want Hallie to know."

"You think she won't? You think you can hide the way your eyes light up when I look at you, when I touch you?"

"Oh, Fletch." She drew in a ragged breath as his hand slid beneath her shirt and closed over her breast. "I don't know. I guess that I didn't think. What are we going to do?"

"Well, you could let me move into the house with you, openly, honestly. Hallie's a big girl now."

Fletcher's idea was mindboggling. She couldn't even consider the implications of such a thought. Silvia Fitzpatrick live openly with a man? For all the world to know? The very thought took her breath away.

"No, Fletcher. I may have come a long way, but I couldn't do that."

"Why? Greg has a lady, someone he cares about, and he's certainly taking a risk with his reputation. The university might not approve. But they haven't fired him and he has more friends than anyone I know. Why not you?"

"Mainly because of Hallie," she said slowly. "Don't you see? I'm still not sure why she came back home. All she's said is that she isn't like those people out there. I can't start behaving irresponsibly in front of my own daughter, even if I were brave enough to want to. Besides, Greg is a man. Anyway, what would my neighbors think?"

"If you mean Honey," Fletch chuckled, turning Silvia's face up so that he could kiss her one last time, "I doubt that she'd be offended. As for Hallie, I can appreciate how you feel about that, though I'm not sure I agree. So, why don't we slip upstairs for a while before you go in."

"Upstairs? You mean make love in the apartment?"

"Unless you'd rather try the backseat of your station wagon." He was pressing against her, planting little kisses down her neck and across her breasts.

"No! I mean, we can't. I mean, making love at Kris's house was one thing, but not here, not where John and I—I . . . I can't. I'd feel guilty."

Silvia tore herself from the sweet torture of his embrace and ran across the yard and onto the porch, slamming the screen door behind her. She stood, gulping frantically, trying to still the roar of her heartbeat.

"Well, I can see you had an interesting weekend, Mother." Hallie's voice came through the darkness. She was sitting on the porch swing, where she could and probably *had* watched Fletcher kissing her in the garage.

"What do you mean?"

"Well, you're lucky there wasn't a police officer waiting or you'd have gotten a ticket. Looks like we both turned and ran."

Silvia sank into a chair and forced herself to gain control. So Hallie had seen Fletcher kissing her. The garage was dark, but the light from Honey's porch filtered through the hedge. Besides, there was no disguising the emotional state she was in.

"What happened with Jeff?"

"It was wonderful, at first. We were—together. No, what that means is that we made love. We didn't leave the hotel room Friday night and Saturday, except for his practice sessions. It was better than it ever was before. He wanted me to come back. I . . . I agreed."

"You did?"

"Then, this afternoon, during the game, he got hurt—again—and I almost died watching him roll around the field in pain. Everything was suddenly back like it was. He was out there killing himself—for the glory. I don't want to see him hurt. And I don't want to fight with him about it anymore. The arguing, the awful, awful fighting. I left."

"Oh, Hallie, I'm so sorry." Silvia stood and sat down in the swing beside her child, taking her into her arms. "I understand about arguing, about the consequences of fighting, more than you'll ever know."

"You see," Hallie went on, sobbing, digging her head into her mother's shoulder, "there's Charlie. I can't let him grow up and see that. I want him to have the kind of life I had: calm, stable, loving. That's what's important."

"Yes, that's what's important. But, Hallie, what about you, your wants?"

"I'll manage, Mother. One way or another, just like you did."

"Just like I did," Silvia repeated, and closed her eyes in dismay. Hallie couldn't know what she was saying. She couldn't know what it meant to manage alone, to be alone. Somehow Silvia had to do something to prevent that happening.

But what?

She couldn't even run her own life. She was

here in her house, when the man she wanted was only fifteen feet away and she couldn't bring herself to close the distance between them.

Lordy, what a mess.

Now Hallie wanted to be just like her.

Four days later Fletcher knocked on Greg's door and waited, rocking impatiently back and forth on the balls of his feet.

"Come."

"All right, Greg Evans, you got me into this, now you're going to have to help get me out. I have to have another place to live."

Greg looked up in surprise. "But I thought you and Silvia were getting along so well."

"Silvia and I *are* getting along very well. That's the problem."

"I don't understand. You'd better explain."

"You don't understand? Old buddy, I don't understand. But I think it goes something like this. Silvia lives in the same house that she lived in when she and John were married. She sleeps in the same bed, the same bed that she used to sleep in when she and John lived in the garage. John's gone, but Hallie's come back and Silvia seems to think that she's been given another chance to right every mistake she ever made."

"What does that mean? I suppose we'd all like a second chance. Wouldn't *you*?"

"Maybe, and maybe it would work. But every place I go in that damned house is full of John. You'd think he was some kind of saint. Hell, he was only a kid. I don't understand."

"I never knew John," Greg answered. "But I understand that he was a bit of a rebel. But that's been," he paused as he counted, "fifteen years ago. Hallie was a child when I first taught Silvia."

"I don't understand it, Greg. But I want out. I want another place, where Silvia and I can be together."

"Oh, I see." Greg struck a match and touched it to his pipe, drawing until a weak curl of smoke rose from the bowl. "You want a neutral zone for you and Silvia to play house in. What does Silvia have to say about that?"

"Hell, I don't know. We spent last weekend at Kris Killian's ranch. Everything was great. Now suddenly she's having doubts. If John's ghost wasn't enough, there's Hallie, there's her reputation. You know Silvia, she's no liberated woman— yet. We can't be together; the neighbors might see; one of the other faculty members might come in; Hallie might discover us."

Greg puffed on his pipe and frowned. "I see. You know I really am pleased, Fletch. Though I hoped, I never thought that Silvia would appreciate a man like you. She's always seemed too level-headed to let herself go. Well, that just goes to prove that you can never predict human nature."

Fletcher stood up, paced back and forth, and flopped down in the chair by his friend's desk. "So, what do I do about Silvia?"

"What do you want to do, Fletcher?"

"One minute I want her so much that I don't even understand it. The next minute I want to get as far away as I can. I feel as if I've stepped into the middle of a Faulkner novel. Moonlight and magnolias, sex and seething passion. At least on Hario Splendor, you could be what you are without being censored. Don't laugh, Greg, but I think I'm a bit scared. I don't want to be away from her at all."

"This may be a surprising suggestion, my friend," Greg said, "but have you ever considered marrying Silvia?"

There was a long, very long, very silent pause.

"Marry? Me, Spider Malone, get married? Why would I want to do that?"

"Oh, I don't know. You just look like a man ready to stand still."

"And do what?"

"Just what you said—be with someone. You're doing so well with the students, I could probably get you a place on the staff. You could write here, put down roots."

"Roots? You must be out of your mind. Why on earth would I pick a place like Athens, Georgia, to put down roots? What would my readers think?"

"It was just a thought."

"I'd go crazy. Maybe, just maybe Fletcher Sims could fit in. But Spider Malone is a man who has to be free. He has to live the adventures I write about. I couldn't do it. Roots? Suppose I lost it all?"

"Lost what, Fletcher? That's what you have to decide. Well, like I said, it was just an idea."

"A damned bad one, Greg. If, and mind you I'm only saying *if*, I ever get married, I'd want somebody who knows the ropes, somebody who can put up with me as I am, who'd love me enough to go where I go. I couldn't ask Silvia to do that. She really is an old-fashioned girl, Greg."

"I can see where you would never fit with an old-fashioned girl, Fletch. Of course there's one benefit—with her you wouldn't have to worry that she'd want to have children to be complete, like . . ." His voice trailed off for a moment before he caught Fletcher's frown and continued. "Old bachelors like us don't need children anyway."

Greg stood and walked over the coat rack, searching for and pulling a fresh pouch of tobacco from his pocket.

"Children?" Fletcher's quick denial died in his throat. He didn't know whether he shared Greg's opinion or not. In truth, he wasn't even certain that Greg was fully convinced of what he'd just said. Fletcher had never consciously thought about being a father until he met Charlie.

Greg sat back down, tapped his pipe on the ash tray, and dumped the ashes out. He refilled the bowl and tamped the tobacco down. "It was just a thought, Fletch. If a new place is what you want, I'll start looking. In the meantime, you can always use mine—if Silvia's willing."

"If Silvia's willing to do what?" Silvia stood in the doorway, waiting, resigned to learning what new venture Greg was planning which would throw her and Fletcher together. "I would have knocked, but the door was open."

"Silvia, come in." Greg rose and waited for

Silvia to enter. "Fletcher and I were just discussing the local customs and mores. Why don't the two of you drive over to Underground Atlanta with Helen and me for their big Halloween party."

"Helen?"

"Yes, Helen Sullivan, the woman I'm engaged to. I thought Fletcher might have mentioned her."

"Oh, Greg," Silvia said sincerely. "Congratulations. I didn't know—that you were getting married, I mean."

"Yeah, well, I gave her every opportunity to change her mind. I was certain that she'd get tired of an old duck like me. You know these younger women."

It was Fletcher's turn to raise a lofty eyebrow. "Younger women, Greg? How old is your lady?"

Greg inhaled nervously and began to cough, covering his unease with the ensuing spasm.

"How old, Greg?" Silvia insisted, slapping Greg on the back.

"She's thirty-five, never been married, no children. She started out as one of my students. Refuses to graduate. We've been—seeing each other for almost a year."

"Well, well, Greg," Fletcher observed with barely contained amusement. "Now I understand at least one of your earlier comments—the one about children."

"Eh, yes, I thought you would. Will you join us for the Halloween celebration, Silvia?"

"Thank you, but I don't think so," Silvia replied quickly.

"Why not? Sure," Fletcher agreed readily,

firmly overruling Silvia. "Silvia and I would like to meet Helen and, frankly, we need to get away from Athens. We'd love to go, wouldn't we, darling?"

"Fletcher!" He was doing it again, answering for her, deciding what she wanted to do without consulting her.

"What time, Greg?" Fletcher went on, moving to Silvia's side.

"We'll pick you up about four, drive over, and have dinner before we take in the activities."

"Good."

Silvia couldn't believe the man. His actions were inexcusable. She wouldn't allow anymore. "Fletcher Sims, I want to talk to you in our office. Now!"

She whirled around and strode down the narrow corridor and into the room at the end. Fletcher lifted his hands palms up to Greg in a gesture that said, *I don't understand women, either*, winked, and set off behind Silvia.

Inside their office he closed the door and turned the lock.

The sound of the lock clicking in place was like a gunshot in the muffled silence.

"What do you think you're doing, Fletcher Malone?"

"I'm locking this door so that we can't be interrupted."

"Why?"

"Because you won't talk about anything important otherwise. Every time I come near you, you jump like you've been shot. You avoid being alone with me. You leave curtains and doors open so that the world is constantly watching. You hide behind Honey, Charlie, Hallie—even Greg. It's been four days since I've touched you and I don't intend to wait another minute."

"Fletcher, don't you come any closer. I came in here because I want us to talk about you making decisions for me, not anything else. Just because Greg Evans is having a midlife crisis doesn't mean *I'm* going to."

"Yes. I made a decision for you. And you can put this discussion on hold for a few minutes, after which you may add another decision I've made for you to your hit list."

"What other decision?"

"This one."

And he was kissing her. She was in his arms, her knees turning to water as the walls began to spin.

"No, Fletcher," she moaned. "We can't."

"Yes we can. Yes we will."

And they did. Right there on the couch in her office in the middle of a lovely October afternoon, Mrs. Silvia Fitzpatrick made passionate love to a traveling man.

This time Fletcher was writing the scene.

The line that came to Silvia's mind was certainly clichéd.

Definitely overused.

But Silvia knew what she felt. It was true after all.

The earth moved.

* * *

"You should have come as a Nightwing," Silvia said as they walked down the cobbled street, through the costumed revelers who'd turned out for the Underground Atlanta Halloween Haunt.

"What's a Nightwing?" Helen Sullivan asked curiously.

"A flirt in feathers," Silvia answered brightly. "A native god who takes the form of a bird to cast his spell over innocent women."

"Pay no attention to Silvia," Greg admonished. "The Nightwing is a figment of Spider Malone's imagination. He uses it as a tool to coerce women and college professors into complying with his wishes."

"Well, I wish I'd brought it along. I'm hungry," Fletcher complained, "and you don't seem to be inclined to feed me."

They'd wandered around, enjoying the costumes worn by the Halloween partygoers. Silvia and Helen insisted on poking about in the little shops, examining the street merchants' wares displayed on everything from carts fashioned from old fire trucks to a farmer's wagon. The city fathers who'd refurbished the old buildings and the old streets that ran beneath the city of Atlanta had done an outstanding job of creating something very special.

But more than the ambience of the underground, Silvia felt a warm glow of happiness at the sharing, the *esprit de corps* of the four of them. She'd never double-dated before. When she and John were together, it was a deliberate secretive aloneness. She didn't fit with his fraternity friends and he didn't fit with her high school activities. Their families had nothing in common, and outside of the breathlessness of touching, kissing, and finally making love, she and John had few shared interests.

Then afterward she'd had Hallie. The three of them were limited to trips to Hurricane Shoals where they picnicked at the remains of the old mill, waded in the creek that plunged over the slippery rocks. Then John was gone and it had been only her and her child. Then Hallie was gone and the dates she'd had were merely two people attending a common event. She'd never intended to close men out of her life. Silvia had only allowed herself to be friends.

"Here we are," Greg announced gaily. "Our destination."

"Where exactly *are* we, old buddy?"

They were standing in one of the alleys, beside a building with no door.

"Dante's Down the Hatch. We have reservations for dinner."

"Fine, darling," Helen agreed with an exaggerated, patronizing air. "Where is Dante's Down the Hatch?"

"Where else?" Greg laughed, grabbing her hand. "Down the hatch." He led the skeptical group into what appeared to be an air vent on the sidewalk. The vent was, in fact, a set of swinging doors which concealed steps leading down.

Fletcher laughed and pulled Silvia to his side, leaned down, and followed.

"I've always thought Greg was a little like the

Mad Hatter," she observed tartly, "now I'm sure of it."

"Be careful of the alligators," Greg called over his shoulder.

At the foot of the steps they found themselves on the wharf, overlooking the moat. The burly man who greeted them introduced himself as Dante and welcomed Greg. Once he found out he was hosting the creator of Spider Malone, he deviated in his direction and seated them in one of the choice locations on the ship's balcony overlooking the band below.

"There were alligators down there," Helen squealed.

"What do you feed them, Mr. Dante?" Silvia asked with a shiver.

"Just Dante, please. What do they eat? An occasional drunk, boring people, hecklers. You don't have to worry," Dante said with a laugh. "Fletcher Sims? Spider Malone, piece of cake. Enjoy."

And they did. The food was superb, the crowd noisy, and little by little, Silvia found herself leaning closer to accept Fletcher's constant touching. When he spoke she turned her cheek to his lips, telling herself that she couldn't hear over the noise of the partygoers. They finished their meal with Dante's famous chocolate fondue and wandered back into the alley where impromptu dancers were enjoying the music streaming from the restaurants.

When Fletcher asked Silvia to dance, she moved into his arms, allowing the pulse of the music to flow through them as if they were one being.

"Ah, Silvia, it ought to be like this all the time," he whispered. "Us in your little kitchen, making breakfast, making late-night snacks, making music with our bodies."

"Fletcher, why do you say things like that? You don't have to use pretty words to seduce me. I'm yours."

"I can't help myself. I want to touch you. I want to see that beautiful face in the morning when your eyes are still filled with sleep, after we've made love all the long, beautiful hours of the night."

"Oh, Spider, you do know how to weave a spell," Silvia whispered, allowing herself to be drawn willingly into his web. Halloween, a night of fantasy. All Hallow's Eve—a time when spirits move through the night, a time for Nightwings and creepy, crawly things that spin webs and snare their innocent prey.

"Let's get out of here," Fletcher said.

"But what about Greg and Helen?"

"They have their own plans, darling." Fletcher inclined his head to the mass of strangers swirling around them. "Greg and Helen will be making music of their own. We'll catch up with them later."

The city streets were noisy. As they walked arm in arm in the warm October-night air, Silvia felt as though it were she who was wearing the disguise. Assistant Professor Silvia Fitzpatrick had been left behind. The woman with Fletcher Malone was a new being, hatched from some enchanted seed which metamorphosed into a spirit that was free and eager to reach for the forbidden ecstasy that Fletcher promised.

She didn't ask where they were going. For tonight, she didn't care. They were together. She leaned against him, resting her head on his arm, matching her steps to his.

"Oh, Fletcher," she whispered, moving her hand to the base of his neck, playing with the muscles in his neck, planting little kisses in the hollow beneath his chin.

"God, woman . . ." He turned, pulling her into the doorway of an office building. "You're going to be ravished in the middle of Peachtree Street if you aren't careful."

She kissed him, over and over again, calling his name between kisses, "Fletcher, Fletcher. I don't want to be careful. I've been careful half my life."

Taking her hand, he pulled her up the street, past the tall new office towers, past Macy's department store with its brightly lit windows decorated like a South Seas island, and into the Peachtree Plaza Hotel.

"Fletcher!" Silvia stopped and looked around. "What are you doing? What about Greg and Helen?"

"Greg made his own reservation, darling. This is for us."

"You mean you had this planned?"

Silvia's heart pounded as she looked at the man who was holding her hand. His blue eyes were swimming with passion. His dark hair was mussed where she'd run her fingers through it.

He exhaled sharply. "Don't you want to make love with me, Silvia?"

Silvia felt her face flush. Didn't she want to make love with this man? Wasn't that what she'd wanted all night, all week, ever since the first time he'd kissed her on her porch. Hadn't that been what she'd planned when she'd taken him to Kris's ranch?

"Oh, yes," she said in a strained voice. "I want that very much."

He held her close while they checked in. He kissed her in the elevator. In the corridor outside the room he unbuttoned her blouse and planted wicked little kisses along the edge of her bra. By the time their door was open the blouse was unbuttoned and falling to the floor. One piece of clothing after another followed until they were both nude.

"You should have worn a costume," Fletch murmured. "You'd be a witch. This time it's me who's caught in a spell."

A bubble of laughter rose in Silvia's throat. The idea of Fletcher being caught in her spell was provocative, heady, altogether too delicious. She laughed again.

"Oh, Fletcher, what have you done to me?"

"Nothing yet, darling. But I'm about to." And he did. With heated fingers and persuasive lips he loved her. Blowing softly into her ear, he whispered words of love that she never expected to hear again. And she teased this man with her body and her soul.

Fletcher left a train of kisses down her body,

across her breasts, down her stomach. His mouth was the instrument of his desire, teasing, searching, luring her into a mindless state of passion.

And then he was kissing her in a place where she'd never felt the sensation of a man's lips before. Moistening, stroking, magnifying the heat of her yearning until she felt as if she were going to explode.

"No, Fletcher. Stop. What are you doing? Please. Please." But the please had turned into a plea, for she never wanted this to end. "Oh, Fletcher, I feel as if I'm flying. Higher and higher . . ." At that moment she felt her body shatter into waves of glowing aftershocks and she lost her last hold on reality.

As the sensation began to subside, she felt Fletcher cover her with his body. Aroused, breathing heavily, he raised himself above her.

"Do you want me, Silvia? Say you want me, my darling."

"Yes. Oh, yes, always."

When he entered her, she accepted his need and rose to meet him thrust for thrust. Over and over, as the longing began to rise again, he whispered her name. "Silvia, Silvia, my love, my love."

This time, when the flood of sensation came it swept over both of them like some thundering tide of heat and fire, bringing them to the mountaintop, then sliding sweetly away, leaving them spent and exhausted.

Fletcher rolled over, holding her half across his body, cradling her in his arms. He caressed her arm, her shoulder, and the side of her face as if he were reassuring himself that she was still there.

"Ah, darling," he whispered, "you sure know how to brew a wicked potion. I think that it's not only powerful, but it's addictive."

"Mmm." Silvia didn't want to talk. All she wanted to do was feel.

"What are we going to do about it?"

"About what?"

"About being together, Silvia?"

"Fletcher, I always thought it was the woman who wanted to talk after making love. The man is supposed to roll over and go to sleep."

"Not this man. I don't want to waste a minute with you. The way things have been going, I may have to wait another week before I'll be able to touch you again."

"You? Not touch me for a week. I don't believe it."

"Speaking of touching, why don't you, Silvia?"

"Why don't I do what?"

"Touch me?"

"I don't know. Touching someone doesn't come natural. I guess because nobody ever touched me, except for Hallie."

"Your mother?"

"My mother died almost before I could remember, and my father . . . ? He was a rough man. My grandfather didn't know how to cope with a teenager. Then there was John."

Fletcher didn't have to hear John's name to know that Silvia had thought of her husband. He could feel it as her body went stiff and tight.

"Tell me about John," he said softly, cuddling her as he tried to reassure her with his touch.

"He was a good boy—man. He tried very hard to be a husband and father. He just didn't know how. And I made it so very difficult for him. I didn't know how to be a wife and mother."

"Who does? Maybe there ought to be a set of instructions issued with the marriage license. Maybe if my mother had read them she wouldn't have made my father's life such a hell that he left."

"Your father left your mother?"

Fletcher wished he hadn't spoken. Bringing his own past into their bed surprised him. Why in the world had he said that? He'd come to terms with his globe-trotting father and his hellfire and damnation mother long ago.

"Yes," he finally admitted. "I suppose you'd say that. He was a military man who spent all his time overseas. My dear mother used to say that he was really a CIA agent who started wars just so that he'd have an excuse to go again."

"Your mother said that? Didn't she love your father?"

"Yes, I think she did. I never thought much about it, but maybe underneath all that righteousness, maybe she did. She gave him all the love she had because there sure as hell wasn't any left over for me."

"I'm sure you're wrong, Fletcher. Every mother loves her child. Perhaps she just didn't know how to show it."

There was a long silence.

Fletcher let his hand slide off Silvia's shoulder.

She felt the strains of rejection, not in his touch, but in the absence of it. Of course. It made sense. That's why Fletcher was always touching people. He was taking what he wanted and was deprived of: approval, affection—love.

She could understand what must have happened. His mother had been abandoned, left by the man she loved, with a child who had learning difficulties, difficulties that made him frustrated and rebellious. How sad. How very sad. Greg Evans had taught Fletcher to deal with his learning problem. But nobody had ever repaired the damage to his soul.

Silvia had spent her life trying to help others, knowing in some way that every small success she achieved erased one of her own failures. Now she was faced with a hurt that went so deep that she didn't know how to begin to ease the pain. Fletcher was right. She cared too much.

Perhaps there was no changing the past. Perhaps she could only help him heal the pain as he learned to accept it. Not with words, but with touching. Shyly, she slid her leg across Fletcher's body. Her hand began a slow, light examination of his chest, rubbing his nipples, drawing little circles down his chest, lining his rib cage.

No response.

In desperation she turned her lips to his body. Lightly, with shy inexperience, she followed the path of her fingertips with her mouth.

"What are you doing, Silvia?"

"I'm touching you, Fletcher Sims, healing you with my lips. Do you feel it? Can't you feel the pain slipping away? Your mother loved you. She just didn't know how to stop the pain. Your father loved you, too. There was nothing you could do then and nothing you can do now. Except learn to stop hurting."

"I can't, Silvia. Just like you can't stop loving John. Perhaps if I hadn't been so rotten she'd still be alive. I was responsible for part of her pain. There is no way you could ever understand that."

"Oh yes I can, Fletcher, I understand far too well. You see . . ." She stopped kissing him as she reached the thick swirl of hair below his navel. "You see, I was a shrew, and my sharp tongue killed my husband. I thought I'd never feel anything again. I tried to stop it from happening, but you made me feel desire."

Fletcher heard the sound of her breathing. He felt the warmth against his body as she exhaled. Her breasts were pressed against his arm. The sweet smell of their lovemaking filled his nostrils.

"Silvia . . ." he began.

"No. Don't talk. Just feel, Fletcher. Maybe we both need to be touched."

Her lips moved down. She would give him pleasure, just as he had given her. She touched, caressed, moistened, and drew on him until he could no longer deny his desire. Hands lying dormant came back to life and returned her caresses, clasping and pressing his fingertips into her flesh until she felt that she was absorbing his pain with her very skin.

"Silvia," Fletcher cried out at last, lifted her into the air and brought her down, imprisoning her on that part of him which was throbbing with release even as they came together.

Later they slept, both cleansed of the burdens of past guilt and hidden longing. Fletcher had covered the world, but his childhood had always been an unwanted quest in every spot he visited. Silvia had never been anywhere, but her guilt had shaped her life.

Tonight perhaps they'd faced the dragons of their past.

Tomorrow? It was too early to think beyond tonight. In each other's arms they'd sleep the sleep of sated passion. Tonight was all there was. All there could ever be, all Silvia ever wanted.

Fletcher Sims was still Spider Malone.

And Spider Malone was a traveling man.

That was the way it had to be.

EIGHT

"You know you could have warned me, Fletcher. I'd have brought a toothbrush."

"There's one in the bathroom, compliments of the hotel. If I'd told you that we had a reservation to spend the night at the Peachtree Plaza, you would never have come, my little puritan."

Silvia stretched beneath the sheet and looked guiltily at their clothing on the floor, now wrinkled and trod upon. What would Greg think? What would Helen think?

"I know," Fletcher echoed her thoughts. "What will Greg and Helen think? That is what you're worrying about, isn't it?"

"Yes, I suppose."

"Well, don't. They're probably thinking that we're as happy as they are, as much in . . ." He cut off the rest of his sentence, swallowing the word love in shock. He'd never told a woman that he loved her. He'd never even come close. Why now?

". . . trouble," Silvia finished his sentence, knowing that wasn't what he had been about to say, knowing that even considering the word he'd swallowed took them in a direction that she wouldn't consider.

But this time Fletcher didn't soothe over his near faux pas. Instead he sat up on the side of the bed for a moment. While his back was turned, Silvia slipped from beneath the sheet, gathered up her clothes, and fled into the bathroom. She ran the shower water, brushing her teeth as it got hot. A few minutes later she was in, out, and dressed. There was nothing she could do about the wrinkles in her clothes, but at least she was ready to leave.

Fletcher was still sitting on the bed when she returned to the room. He was talking on the phone.

"Sure, brunch at the Top of Peachtree will be fine, Greg. We'll meet you in an hour. I think that Silvia and I will go downstairs and slip into Macy's for a quick shopping trip first."

He put down the phone and glanced up at Silvia. This time it was Fletcher who was uncomfortable.

"I thought you might like a new dress or something. I'm afraid that yours got kind of wrinkled last night."

"Thank you. I would."

Silvia knew that it wasn't going to be easy for either of them. She turned her back and walked over to the dressing table where she'd laid her purse. At least she could comb her hair. In the mirror she watched as Fletcher stood and walked into the bathroom, stopping to retrieve his underwear and T-shirt.

He didn't try to hide his nudity. But then, he was probably accustomed to walking about in front of his lady loves. If Silvia's own appreciation was any indication, they probably enjoyed him more without clothes. They probably enjoyed everything about the man, just as much as she did.

Silvia straightened her back. This was ridiculous. They'd just made love, slept together, awakened in each other's arms. Why was she embarrassed, filled with guilt? Hallie wasn't here, and Greg and Helen were about to be married. Besides, who would know and why should anybody care?

"Silvia! I've got the answer."

Fletcher burst through the door, wrapping a towel around his waist, and caught Silvia to him, whirling her around in joyful exuberance. "You and I are getting married!"

"What?"

"You heard me. We're going to be married."

"You're doing it again, Fletcher Sims, making decisions for me. We are most certainly *not* getting married. That's the most foolish thing I've ever heard of."

She could barely breathe, he was holding her so tightly. Beads of water were rolling down his face and splattering on her blouse. His fierce expression might have stopped her protest. His grip on her shoulders might have slowed her anger. But when he kissed her she forgot every word she would have said.

When he'd taken her breath away, and thoroughly convinced her that she should never again question his authority, he stopped his assault on her lips and said, "And don't you ever use the word foolish about us again."

"All right." That was all she could manage.

"Now listen up. I don't know how it will work, but we're going to be married. I'm giving up Spider Malone. I'll get a job just like everyone else and we'll be a regular family. I know that you're a career woman. You've already raised one child and you probably won't want more, and I'll live with that. It'll work. We'll make it work. How does a Christmas wedding sound?"

"Fletcher, slow down," Silvia said softly. "You don't know what you're saying. This is foo— out of the question. You would never be happy living in Athens, Georgia. As for Spider Malone, he's much too young to die."

"Don't you . . . want to marry me, Silvia?"

Silvia willed her eyes to remain dry, her voice to be steady and calm. "No, Fletcher, I don't think that would be a good idea. John and I thought we were in love and we got married. I still don't know whether it was love, or desire. But I won't do that to you."

"Sex? You think that's what this is about?"

"I don't know, Fletcher. But what we have is good. And I . . . I do want to be with you. So, for as long as you're here, I won't say no anymore."

Fletcher looked at her proud face, the open

expression of her feelings. She'd come a long way from that first morning. Facing her desire and agreeing that she wanted him in her bed was proof of her feelings. But somehow that didn't make him feel good about it. He didn't want her to be a woman of today—open and honest. The shy, proper lady he'd first met was special and he wasn't certain that he approved of the new one.

What kind of man was he? He'd changed a woman into what he wanted; now he wanted her to be what she'd been.

"About those clothes . . . I hope that you're going to pay for them," she said shyly. "If I'm going to be a kept woman, I expect to be kept very well."

"All right," Fletcher agreed, still stunned by the change of direction their relationship had taken. "I've never taken a lady shopping. I guess there's a first time for everything. This will be a new experience for Spider Malone."

Shopping with Spider Malone was a new experience for Silvia, too. By the time they'd finally outfitted them both from the skin out, they were already twenty minutes late for brunch and they'd managed to put Fletcher's unexpected marriage proposal behind them.

Silvia's counterproposal was easier to deal with because while they might try to put their night of being close behind them, their bodies refused.

Greg and Helen didn't comment on Fletcher and Silvia's new open expressions of affection.

Silvia and Fletcher didn't comment on Greg and Helen's wedding plans. For Silvia the idea of a wedding was a painful reminder of what she'd just rejected. By not extending the conversation she was able to remain outwardly happy.

It was the argument on the return trip of the four that finally put a damper on the day.

"Greg," Helen said sharply, "you are not too old to be a father. So you'll be a retired member of the faculty by the time your son graduates from college, so what?"

"Silvia, explain to this woman that people like us get used to having their lives organized. Can you imagine what a baby would do to my routine? Tell her."

"Why don't I just let you borrow Charlie for a day or so. That'll teach you, real quick."

"Oh, I don't know," Fletcher disagreed. "Having a little one around makes you appreciate the joy of learning. Chasing him down will definitely keep you young."

"Fine," Greg muttered. "Then *you* have a child."

Fletcher frowned and glanced out of the car window. "Who knows, maybe I will."

For the next week Fletcher and Charlie were inseparable during the day. Silvia and Fletcher were inseparable at night. Though she knew she probably wasn't fooling anybody, Silvia couldn't bring herself to admit to their relationship openly. Finding ways to be together was difficult.

Finding ways for Charlie and Fletcher to be together wasn't. When they couldn't convince Silvia to accompany them to the park, they rode off on Fletcher's bike alone. Silvia worried about the relationship. What would happen when Fletcher left? How would Charlie survive losing first his father, then his friend? What was becoming an even bigger problem was how Silvia could survive losing the man who'd filled her life completely.

During the next weeks, Hallie began to insist on helping in the office. In spite of her studies and taking care of Charlie, she still had too much time on her hands. Silvia wasn't the least surprised to discover that Hallie had a talent for the work.

It was just before Thanksgiving when Jeff called again. He couldn't get away, but he wanted very much to see Charlie. Would Hallie bring him to New Orleans for his next game? Silvia hurt for her child when she saw how much she wanted to go and how difficult it was for her to make the decision to refuse.

A surprise invitation to Kris Killian's ranch was the only thing that made the holiday a joyful occasion. Kris's invitation included Hallie and Charlie, Greg, and Helen, the students in Mister Raschad's class of Spider's Boys, as they'd begun to call themselves, even Honey Watts. He didn't want anybody to be alone on Thanksgiving.

There was a rowdy game of touch football, a swim in the indoor part of the pool, and more food than Silvia even wanted to think about. It was while she was watching Fletcher and Charlie in the pool that Silvia realized how much that picture had begun to mean to her. The quarter's end and Fletcher's time to go was drawing close. She couldn't imagine her life without him.

"I hate to think about all this ending. Charlie

will miss Fletcher when he's gone," Silvia said to her daughter, wondering if Hallie had considered the problem.

"What do you mean, Mother? I thought that you and Fletcher might have something, that he might stay."

"No, darling. Fletcher is like some wild, free spirit. This is just a period of hibernation, a time for him to recharge his energy. He'd never be happy here. I wouldn't even want him to try."

"I see. Won't you miss him?"

"Oh, yes. I'll miss him. But I've learned to deal with loss. I lost your father, then you. One thing I have learned is that life changes, but it goes on."

Fletcher, sitting on the ceramic tile at the pool's edge, had been watching Charlie splash in the water with the young athletes. He climbed from the pool and called out, "Go with Mister and get some clothes on, boy, before you turn into a prune."

"Life goes on. But it's hard to change it. That's what I'm learning, too." Hallie repeated Silvia's words. "But I don't think I like it much."

"Neither do I," Fletcher said, dropping to the floor beside the couch where Silvia was sitting. "I've been listening to the two of you, and I think I ought to tell you, Hallie, that I asked your mother to marry me."

"You did?"

"And she turned me down. I'm not sure why, but she did. For almost a month I've been waiting for her to see that we could make it work, but she refused to believe it. I don't know how Jeff let you get away from him, but I sure as hell hope you know what you're doing. Because if you're following in your mother's footsteps, I think you're heading down a long, lonesome road."

"Fletcher!" Silvia stood up, her face drained white with shock. "How dare you say such a thing to Hallie, in front of Kris and Honey! What I do, what *we* do, is private and I don't appreciate you making a public issue of it."

"I see. Nothing is going to change your mind, is it, Silvia? Not even if I tell you in front of all these witnesses that I love you."

She gasped. She hadn't expected that. Still, no matter how much she'd wanted to hear those words, she couldn't allow herself to give in.

"No. I won't marry you. I love you, the man you are—Spider Malone and Fletcher Sims. But if you stayed here you'd change. I can't do that to you. I won't. You'd turn into someone like your father and I'd become a bitter, nagging shrew. No, it won't work."

He stared at her for a long moment. "Fine. Then I guess there's only one thing to do—leave. The quarter's almost over. All I have left to do is see that Mister and his group pass their final exam, then I'm out of here. In the meantime, I'll just sleep on Greg's couch." His voice grew deeper and slower, giving evidence to the fury he was trying to control.

"Fletcher, you don't have to do that," Silvia said softly. "I don't want to send you away."

"Why not, Lady Fitzpatrick, isn't that what

you've been doing from the beginning? I'm sure Kris will get you all home in his van. I'll just take my bike."

"Don't do this, Fletcher. Please!" Silvia pled, her voice in anguish. "Don't leave angry. Something bad could happen to you."

"Something probably will. But I have to go. Good-bye, Silvia. I'm a tough boy. I don't have to deal in the quodilibetic ramblings of a woman who doesn't know what she really wants."

"I don't deal in 'theories and abstractions,' Mr. Sims. I'm as practical as you are. I certainly don't take tramp steamers to some island on the south side of nowhere and hide from life."

"No, my darling, Silvia, you hide right where you are. If you change your mind, I'll be spending Christmas on Hario Splendor, where Santa Claus had better fill Spider Malone's stocking with a new book or I may just turn serious and write a *real* book in my old age."

By the time they got home Fletcher was already gone. Charlie was too sleepy to understand what had happened. But after three days of his missing Fletcher and three nights of Silvia's missing Fletcher, Hallie threatened to send them both to the woodshed for a little discussion.

Silvia didn't know where Fletcher had moved his office, but the cozy room they'd shared was suddenly colder than King Tut's tomb. For the first time she was short-tempered with her students. Even Hallie's long face began to wear on her nerves. Finally, after Hallie had spanked Charlie for the first time since they'd been back home, Silvia realized that something had to be done.

Both of the Fitzpatrick women were missing the men they loved. Silvia knew she couldn't change that until she straightened out the mess in her daughter's life.

With the hope that she wasn't making a mistake, she became an interfering mother and placed a call to Jeff the next day. She was going to tell him that he had to come and get Hallie before it was too late.

She didn't need to tell him. He'd already submitted his resignation from the team. Playing professional football wasn't as important to him as his family. It wasn't playing with pain that he feared, but some kind of permanent injury that would keep him from being a husband and father. Hallie was right to leave him. He was a small-town boy, a small college-town boy and he was coming home. The university had offered him a position working with freshmen receivers. He'd already accepted the job.

"Could we live in your garage apartment for a while?"

"No way," Silvia said emphatically. "You'll live in the house."

"But won't we be in the way?"

"No, Jeff. You won't be in the way at all. I promise."

Silvia hung up the phone and headed for Greg's office. "Is he at your apartment?"

"Not anymore."

"Where is he?"

"About halfway to Miami. He left yesterday, Silvia. I thought you knew."

"No, I didn't." Silvia's throat was tight. She felt her vision blur and her heart beat erratically. She'd waited too long. He was gone.

"I'm just sorry he turned down a permanent position on the staff. He seemed genuinely excited about taking on a teaching career."

"He turned down a job? You mean he really wanted to stay and teach?"

"I thought so. Fletcher was content for the first time since I've known him. He loved the idea of having a family, the family he's been looking for since he was a boy. He was excited about some new writing project about learning disorders. He'd even discussed the idea with his agent. Too bad you couldn't work things out. I never saw two people more in love."

What had she done? Had she been so caught up in living a life of repentance that she was ready to lose the man she loved? Hallie had her own family. Silvia needed Fletcher Sims and she was going after him.

"Greg, do you think you could give my exams? They're already made up. It's just a matter of . . ."

"I think I remember how to give exams, Silvia. Why?"

"Because I won't be here. I'm about to catch a banana boat to the South Seas, and if I'm really lucky, I'm going to live on an island in a very large web."

"And if you're not?"

"Then a little grass shack will just have to do."

* * *

Silvia missed the boat. The helicopter she hired to catch the ship was appropriately black, and tongue-swallowing scary. But she didn't care. After all, she was Spider Malone's lady and she was determined to let herself go.

The helicopter landed on the water near the boat. A small launch collected her and brought her back to the ship where she met a grumbling captain and a cheering crew.

"I hope you know that you've brought this ship to a standstill, lady," he muttered, waving off the helicopter and giving sharp orders to the hands milling about.

"I know, and I'm very sorry. But I had to reach Mr. Sims."

"Don't know why I'm surprised," he grumbled as he called one of the hands to take her below. "Don't think two are going to travel for the price of one."

The cabin was at the end of the narrow hall. Silvia knocked.

"Come."

She opened the door and stepped inside. Fletcher was sitting on his bunk, staring at a laptop computer. He didn't look up. Silvia caught her breath and said a small prayer that she was doing the right thing.

"Exactly what I had in mind, my love," she whispered.

"Silvia!" Fletcher slid the machine to the floor and stood. "What are you doing here?"

"Nothing yet. But I brought my script."

Fletcher was wearing only a pair of running shorts. His chest was bare. He stood and took a step toward her, his eyes riveted to hers. "Oh?"

"It says that heroine confesses that she's head over heels in love with the traveling man who made love to her and left without saying good-bye."

"Without saying good-bye? I think you have a motivation glitch here, darling. I read the same script and the traveling man proposed marriage before he left."

"Yes, he did. But the heroine was scared. She'd spent most of her life trying to make up for the hurt she thought she'd caused, trying to create the kind of home she'd thought she owed her child. She didn't know how to go after what she wanted for herself."

"And she does now?"

"No, but she's trying to learn."

"Ah, Silvia, don't do this unless you're sure. I don't think I could take losing my world again."

"*Our* world, my darling Fletcher. Now, you'd better kiss me or I'll begin to believe that you don't want me."

"The hell you say," he groaned, reaching out and pulling her into his arms. He kissed her, drew back, and frowned at her, then kissed her again, his mouth rough and demanding, his anger just beneath the surface. "Just me and you, lady, from now on."

"Not necessarily, my love."

"What does that mean?" He thrust her from

him, frowning as he asked; "Do you have Greg and Honey and Mister with you?"

"No," she said coyly as she began to remove her clothing. "But I thought we might consider, just consider, mind you, adding real commitment to our plot."

"I don't understand."

"Marriage, darling. The captain tells me that we'll have to do it over when we reach port, but he can still perform a ceremony at sea."

Fletcher swallowed hard. The woman stepping out of her slacks and sliding fresh-colored panty hose down her legs was some kind of self-confident siren. Marriage? Babies? He was having a great difficulty assimilating what he was hearing.

"Greg is putting your teaching job on hold for the rest of the year. I figure if we're going to spend the rest of our lives in my world, it's only fair that we start it in yours. But we have to be back in Athens, Georgia, next September."

By this time she was nude, standing before him with breasts peaked and legs slightly spread. Fletcher's expression was so strained that he seemed to be in pain. Had she been wrong? Was this all a mistake? No, they were two people who'd spent their lives hiding from their pain. But no more. Together they'd turned pain into joy, and she refused to accept any thought of losing that.

"What do you think, lover? Are you fresh out of words?"

"Marriage?" That was the only word in his mind. The woman he loved was offering herself to him, herself and a life of love and joy, and all he could say was marriage?

"But I warn you, Fletcher, I'm used to making my own decisions. I'm not very brave and I worry about what people think about me. I really don't know much about making a man happy. I never learned how. So be sure you know what you're getting into."

Fletcher gazed at her, allowing relief and happiness to flood through him, taking away any doubt and anger he had left. "Oh, Silvia," he said softly, "as long as we love each other, we'll work it out. We have a month on board ship to talk about it."

"Talk? Don't you think we've talked long enough?" She stepped forward, put her hands on the waistband of his shorts, and began to slide them down his body, allowing them to drop unnoticed to the floor.

She was right. They had all their lives to deal with words. For now, their eyes glistened with desire, their hands burned with the need to touch, and their bodies arched against each other to comply.

"No lady would do what you're doing, Silvia," Fletcher finally managed to say.

"No gentlemen would be so reticent about cooperating," she whispered, touching his face with her lips and his soul with her heart. "Don't you want to accept my proposal? It's a once-in-a-lifetime offer."

"I thought you understood, Lady Fitzpatrick, that you're dealing with Spider Malone. One lifetime offer is all I ever want." He lifted her in his arms and took the two steps back to the bed where he answered without hesitation. "I've never told another living soul this truth, Silvia, but this is one spider who interdigitates for life."

Silvia didn't have to look that up. She knew what it meant—entwined forever.

"Fletcher," she asked, much, much later, "once you called me nani momi. I've never found out what that means."

"Nani momi." He drew her closer and kissed her. "That means, beautiful pearl, my treasure."

"Uh huh, and I know how pearls are formed. They're tiny impurities that irritate their host until he closes them off with a hard shell. Don't ever do that to me, Fletcher."

"I promise, Silvia. Nothing will ever come between us, or separate us again. It's the two of us against the world."

"Not necessarily, darling. I think I ought to warn you. I wasn't certain how you'd accept my plan, so I decided when I packed that this time I'd travel light."

"If you mean you only have the clothes on your back, that's probably more than you'll need."

"Not exactly, Fletch. Let's just say I saw how much you cared about little Charlie. We'll make wonderful parents. I think we'd better get to that captain pretty quick."

Fletcher gasped. "Silvia, are you pregnant?"

"Not yet, but I intend to be. Will that make you happy?"

"Deliriously. But tell me one thing . . . You're

not the kind of lover who kills her mate at the moment of conception are you?"

"Are you scared?"

"Not a bit, darling. Remember, it's Spider Malone who provides the action. But it's Fletcher Sims who writes the book. From now on, I only write happy endings."

Spider Malone and Fletcher Sims, a lifetime of fantasy and a future filled with everlasting love. She wouldn't have it any other way.

NINE

The sky over Hario Splendor was pink and purple and gold in the twilight. It was reflected in the clear blue waters of the lagoon, shimmering like a beautiful painting, serene and peaceful to the eye. Little floating islands had been made from vines and greenery, interwoven with flowers and centered with a candle. The swimmers took them out in the ocean and released them to float to shore with the incoming tide.

Silvia was dressed in a white lace flowing gown, borrowed from the wife of the tribal chief. The dress had been worn by another woman, long ago, a woman who had fled a life she could no longer bear and come to the island to live with the man she loved. When she'd been told the story weeks ago, Silvia didn't have to be told that the woman was the chief's wife. She could see it in her eyes every time the elderly couple touched.

Silvia's hair had grown longer on the island. Now it was adorned with a crown of tiny orchids and fragrant white blossoms. Her face, honey colored from long walks in the sun along deserted beaches with the man she loved, now glowed with happiness. She hadn't seen Fletcher all day. Since the festival the night before, they'd been separated. In a mock kidnaping ceremony, she'd been taken to the bride's hut on one side of the village and Fletch had been restrained, guarded by his friends, forced to stay in his house alone.

A gentle breeze swept up from the lagoon and ruffled the fronds of the palm trees surrounding the bride's hut. Silvia was alone now, left to savor the memories of their time together on the island. Hario Splendor was everything she'd ever dreamed a romantic South Seas island to be. The people were gentle and loving, moving freely through their lives without hypocrisy or lies.

There were children everywhere, laughing, happy children who quickly found Silvia and Fletcher to be as giving of their knowledge as the children were of theirs. Silvia had learned about the flowers, the fish, and the legends of the island while the children had proudly spouted their ABC's and even managed to learn to read a few words.

But Silvia found it hard to accept their lack of ambition. There was one small dark-eyed, orphan girl called Luiani who touched Silvia's heart. The girl was quick and eager to learn. Her beauty was evident. Even now at fourteen, she was still a child, although nearly a woman. But there was no future for her on Hario Splendor and Silvia questioned Fletcher about her worries.

"Don't do it, Silvia. The missionaries ruined a happy people by forcing their culture on them. I swore when I came here that I'd never do that."

"But what will happen to her?"

"She'll fall in love with one of the island boys and they'll marry and have their own family."

"But she could have so much more."

Fletcher gave Silvia a searching look. "More? More than us, than what we have together?"

Silvia thought about what she'd said and winced. Fletcher was right. Who was she to make judgments about someone else? She was a woman who almost let commitments come between her and the man she loved more than life itself. Would she give up Fletcher for a career, for success? No, but then realistically she didn't have to. And, looking into her heart, she knew that if the choice had to be made now, she'd stay right here, with Fletcher on Hario Splendor forever.

"No, my darling," she said confidently. "Nothing means more than what we have—nothing."

And now her heart was bursting with excitement. She didn't know what would happen, but she might have been sixteen and meeting the love of her life for the first time the way her pulse was racing.

In the silence the drums began, slowly, softly at first, as if they were keeping pace with the pulse of the island and the closing of the day. She could hear the gentle slap of the waves against the white sand. Muted laughter rose and fell and the shadows deepened.

Across the compound, in a shack constructed on a private inlet, Fletcher waited. He couldn't believe how nervous he was. For the last ten minutes he'd paced the confines of his house until his guards had begun to smile. His wedding garments were hardly what he would have worn in Athens, Georgia, but here on the island he was in his element.

His dark hair curled around his forehead and down the back of the collar of his white shirt. A garland of small red flowers and white ribbons had been arranged on his head. The white shirt was unbuttoned half way and hung loose over white duck pants that were cut off just below the knees. Smaller garlands of flowers were tied around his ankles and the sound of shells tied to the ribbons made little tinkling sounds when he walked.

"When, Moki? When do we get started?"

"Soon, Fletcher, soon the call will come." His young, dark-skinned companion flashed a broad smile and walked to the open window.

"What call? How will we know?"

"Don't worry, my friend. She won't run away and we won't let you be late. Luiani is with her. Relax."

"Relax. How in hell do you expect me to relax. This is—this is probably the most important day in my life and here I am wearing flowers in my hair and bracelets on my feet."

"The flowers are a legendary part of our joining, my friend. They signify life and children and beauty."

"Children?"

Fletcher came to a stop in his pacing. He and Silvia had been together for nearly a month, lying in each other's arms at night, making love on the beach, in the volcanic outcroppings, everywhere. There was not a day when they hadn't been together, not a day when she'd begged off because it wasn't a good time, not a day when she'd pushed him away. Month? No, it had been longer than that that they'd been together.

At first Fletcher smiled. Then he began to laugh. He started out the door, determined to find Silvia, find her and make her confess her secret. He wanted to see the tenderness, the shining of her soul in her eyes. He recalled the secret smiles of her friends as he passed, the lovely giggles of the native women when he took his battered old typewriter and retired to his working room where Spider Malone was on the move again, more outrageous than ever.

Children.

He thought about the implication. Silvia was pregnant. Silvia, the woman he loved beyond anything he'd ever dreamed, was carrying his child.

"Hey, mon, where you going?"

"I have to see Silvia."

But he didn't, for at the moment he stepped on the porch the night silence was broken by a mournful call of some native horn. It sounded again and again, like a great musical note sweeping down from the mountain and out to sea.

"It is time," Moki announced with a nod to the other men waiting beyond the house.

Forming a brigade, the flower bedecked delegation surrounded Fletcher and started down the torch lit path to the water's edge. Bonfires had been built along the beach. Behind the fires, between the shore and the trees sat the drummers and the dancers who kept the rhythm of the beat with their slow sensual movements.

Fletcher felt his heart beat faster. His eyes darted frantically back and forth as they walked. Where was she? Where was Silvia?

Then he saw her.

Like a spirit from the sea she was approaching him from the other direction, surrounded by native girls wearing brightly colored sarongs and flowers in their hair. The sea breeze caught her black hair and tousled it behind her. The same wind ruffled her dress and the ribbons from her crown. She was an illusion, a sea nymph, a dream, and he wanted to push aside his compatriots and run across the sand to take her in his arms.

From the sea came a native boat, decorated with flowers and lights. Its paddlers maneuvered the boat to the shore where a group of the village elders assisted the high priest to the shore.

Fletcher took a quick breath. His heart beat rapidly. The priest was wearing the traditional ceremonial garments of flowered cape and fronds. His headdress was half a man high and woven with bright yellow feathers. In his right hand, he carried a staff.

Just as Fletcher and Silvia met, the priest

stepped forward and spoke. The companions of the bride turned Silvia to face the priest as did those accompanying Fletcher.

Though Fletcher understood enough of their language to guess at the words, Silvia would have been lost, except that Luiani had tried to explain what would happen.

The high priest began to chant, creating a kind of spell with his deep melodious voice. The drums and the dancers took up the hum until it seemed to vibrate from the very ground on which Silvia and Fletcher stood, side-by-side, not touching, yet feeling the other's presence more vividly than touch would have expressed.

Beyond the priest, the sea swirled in little white ruffled waves that moved less smoothly now, as if it had changed its mind and was beginning to retreat. The little islands of flowers and light moved out, then back, then out again, as the ocean was caught between the change of tides, forming a lovely display of synchronized movement. Silvia felt as if she was enclosed in a world of beautiful light and sensual fragrance. She moistened her lips and took a deep breath.

Fletcher watched her absorb the wonder of the night and the ceremony. The energy of the dancers and the drums seemed to undulate the very air and all their senses were enriched. Beyond the horizon, the first star of the evening appeared and the sky darkened in respect. Never in his life had he been so moved. When the priest took Fletcher's hand and joined it with Silvia's he felt as if his being was now complete.

"Man was created from the spirit of the volcano, as was woman. They were thrown from deep within the earth into the sky and back to the land again where they were nurtured by the mother sun and the father moon."

The natives chanted a reply.

"Now the great mother and father bring these two mortals together, joining them forever as one being before all who came before and all who are yet to come." The chanting voices repeated the words.

"Will you, Silvia, live with and love with this man for all your days to come?"

"Yes."

"Will you, Fletcher, live with and love with this woman for all your days to come?"

"Yes."

The rapture was so complete that for a moment Silvia and Fletcher didn't realize that the priest had lapsed into words with which they were familiar.

"Now, by the power vested in me, by the island gods, and as a legal, authorized official of the government of the island of Hario Splendor, I now declare that you are man and wife. You may kiss your bride."

"Now you kiss bride," Moki prompted in a loud whisper.

"Finally," Fletcher said under his breath, "the part I understand."

His arms slipped around her and for a very long time he simply held her. Words failed him now, instead he spoke his feelings with his gentle touch and eyes filled with love.

She lifted her proud face to him. How unbelievably sweet it felt to claim her lips, to feel her body trembling beneath his hands, to know that this moment was theirs alone. They kissed as two people who understood that they had forever, slowly, gently, releasing their hold and parting, because they knew that this was only the promise of what was to come.

They turned, broad smiles inching across both their faces as they recognized and accepted the sharing of their love with their friends.

"Now, we feast," Moki said and gave a shrill yell.

The drums immediately changed beat and the dancers formed a corridor through which the bride and groom walked. At the edge of the trees two seats had been fashioned from logs covered with flowers. Fletcher and Silvia were to occupy the marriage throne for the remainder of the festivities. Hand in hand, they watched as the dancers demonstrated with their swirling hips and graceful hands the joining ceremony and what was to come.

With suggestive yells they were joined by the young men of the tribe, whose dancing was openly seductive as they teased the women and danced away again without touching.

"And I thought it was the women who teased," Silvia said with a shake of her head.

"Not here, darling. The men of Hario Splendor

aren't guilty of fabulation in courtship. They're totally honest about their desire."

"Fabulation? The inventing of fantastic tales?" She watched as Luiani reached out and touched Moki openly the next time he moved within range. She noted the surprised expression on Moki's face and the effort he made to dance his way back to Luiani. "I'd say that applies to us women, too."

"Oh? Care to give me a demonstration?"

Silvia gave her new husband a wicked look. "Why not?" She left her chair and joined the women on the floor, rotating her hips as Luiani had instructed her, moving her feet slowly up and down. Her hands gracefully telling the story of her need, while her eyes spoke her desire.

Fletcher gasped. He couldn't believe that this beautiful, sensual woman was the same person who refused to ride his motorcycle because of what people would say. She was talking now, with every cell of her body, before the entire population; she was saying that she wanted him.

The music ended and the women sank to the sand, prostrating themselves on the sand, their arms extended toward the man for whom they were dancing.

Fletcher stood. His breath came short and fast. "Silvia."

She rose and walked toward him, holding out her hand. When he accepted it, she stepped forward, planting her back to his chest as she pulled his arms around her waist.

"The native men obviously have learned control, darling. You're going to have to work on that."

"What?" Fletcher's thoughts were spinning.

"Control, darling. I don't think those little sarongs the men wear are very secure. If they react as you have, they might be embarrassed." She gave a little backwards thrust.

"Oh." He was very aroused, very hard. And he'd stood up, before the natives, for the world to see. He flinched, then considered the situation. "Hell, I don't care. So I want you, there's nothing wrong with that. This is the island of love and we're newlyweds. What do you say we slip away and find a spot—"

"Not yet, darling," Silvia scolded. "First comes the feast, then more entertainment, then—well, that's as far as I got in my instructions."

"Who gave you those instructions?"

"Luiani."

"Well, what can you expect from a fourteen year old? She can't possibly know about making love."

"She knows. In fact, she started to explain what I should expect on my honeymoon, but I told her that I didn't need that kind of instruction."

Fletcher moved one hand lower, capping her stomach possessively. She felt so good. Everything about holding her felt good and right.

"What are you doing, Fletcher?"

"Just holding you, my wife, mother of all my children."

"All your children? Fletcher, I'm almost thirty-six years old. How many do you have in mind?"

"I'm not worried about numbers," he chuckled. "I'm content to accept what comes."

"I hope you know what you're in for. Crying babies, spitting up, sleepless nights, it can be a shock."

"Silvia, my darling wife, there's nothing Spider Malone can't handle. Besides, we have Hallie around to give advice."

The wedding feast consisted of roast pig, fresh fruits, vegetables, and homemade wine. Silvia expected to hear the movie director call, "That's a wrap," any minute. She picked at the food, counting the minutes until the celebration was over and she and Fletcher could steal away. One by one, the little islands of flowers had been swept out to sea as the tide changed. The bonfires burned low and the drums were put aside.

Just as Fletcher was convinced that the end had come, there was a sudden flurry and the two contingents of escorts burst into the clearing carrying a real, true to life, wedding cake, ablaze with candles.

"What?" Fletcher was dumbfounded.

"How on earth?" Silvia began.

"We are not backward," Moki explained. They'd arranged by radio to have the cake baked at the resort hotel on a distant island. It was flown by sea plane to a neighboring island and their best paddlers picked it up at night and stored it in the cool cave beneath the water's level. It was Hario Splendor's gift to Silvia and Fletcher Sims.

Tears streamed down Silvia's face as she cut the cake. She gave a slice of cake and a kiss to every single resident of the island. Afterward, she cut a large piece and walked to the water's edge.

"For the spirit of the sea that brought us here," she said and dropped the cake into the water.

The natives sighed. Their voices began to chant in unison. Fletcher and Silvia took their own share of cake and followed the pathway, lighted by the hand-held torches of the native men and women. Up the beach, through the trees to a newly constructed hut, built just for them, away from the others.

"This is for you and you alone," Moki explained. "After you leave, it will be destroyed and never used again. Only the spirits of those who have gone before you will use this place. It is yours for as long as you choose."

And suddenly they were alone.

The moon rose full and bright overhead, illuminating the clearing and their faces. He listened to the spirit of the wind as it danced among the leaves. He heard the sound of her heart beating steadily in the silence. The fragrance of their flowers was heady in the night air.

There was desire, but there was so much more. He wanted to tell her that she made him feel still and calm inside; that she made him want to do good things to make her proud. She made him afraid that he couldn't make her happy. Where were the words? He couldn't seem to find them. Instead he simply stood, drinking in the sight of her.

"I'm so glad you found me, Fletcher Sims. You brought me back to life again."

"Silvia, my wife," he said, taking her in his arms, burying his face in her hair. For a long time he held her, not moving, not speaking. Then he pulled back and kissed her forehead, her eyelids, her nose, and finally, her mouth.

She opened herself to him, pressing against him, whispering, between kisses, words that had no meaning.

Then he lifted her and carried her inside. More candles lit the palm leaf shack. On the floor lay a cotton pallet, sprinkled with flower petals. Laying her on the fragrant bed he stood, removing his clothes, never taking his eyes from her. Then he knelt beside her. Silvia sat up and began to unfasten the tiny buttons at her back.

"Let me," Fletcher said in a tight voice.

His fingers were clumsy. They trembled as he worked, but Silvia offered no assistance. When he finally completed his task he lifted the dress and pulled it over her head. Beneath it, she was completely nude.

Fletcher gasped. She was beautiful the night they made love in Kris's pool, but there was a luminous tone to her skin now that glowed beneath his touch. She was so very special, this woman he'd married, this woman who would bear his child. He took one of her nipples into his mouth and felt her immediate response. He kissed her breasts, teased, touched, and was rewarded by soft moans of pleasure.

And then, like the incoming tide, it came, the fire of desire that swept over them. His kisses deepened, his touch became more demanding, more insistent. Silvia felt herself caught up in the heat of the candle flame which was only a pale reflection of her own desire, giving touch for touch, movement for movement.

Then Fletcher stopped. He lifted his head, listening as if someone were calling him.

"What's wrong?"

"Wrong," he answered, turning back to her with a smile, "nothing's wrong. Everything is right. Don't you feel it?"

She forced herself to still the erotic beat of her pulse. Her breathing evened and the feeling of warmth swept over her. "Yes."

"The spirits of other lovers," Fletcher said confidently. "I'm being told to slow down, to make this moment beautiful for both of us."

He laid down beside her, pulling her close to him, positioning her head on his arm and her leg across his thighs. "I want this to be special, Silvia."

"There's no way it can't be special, Fletcher, unless it doesn't happen. I don't think the spirit world expects us to lie here like brother and sister. I rather believe that they feel what I feel, which, my darling husband, is very frustrated."

She raised up, planting little butterfly kisses across his chin, down his neck and across his chest. "You know, you're a very beautiful man, Fletcher Sims. I like the way you feel here," her fingers rimmed his nipples, danced down his chest and found his navel before dipping lower. "And here, this portion of your body is pretty spectacular, too. Of course, I haven't had a great deal to compare it with, but I suspect that you're right up there with the champions."

Fletcher groaned, raised up and thrust her back against the flower strewn covering. The scent of crushed blossoms perfumed her body. The silkiness of her skin inflamed his mind and he caressed her wildly, expressing his love in every movement. And then he moved over her and she sighed in satisfaction.

He was heavy against her. She liked that. She liked feeling him covering her, his arousal caught between them, maddeningly close but not yet connected to that part of her that was straining to reach him. He took her face in his hands.

"I love you, Silvia Fitzpatrick Sims, with every part of my being."

"And I love you, Fletcher Sims," she replied without hesitation, "but if you don't hurry, I'm going to look for Spider Malone. He's a man who knows when a woman is dying for want of a lover."

"Fletcher Sims and Spider Malone are one and the same, my darling wife, and this man knows very well how to satisfy his woman."

And then he was inside her, moving with her, giving himself, and taking what she was giving in return. There was no more Spider, Fletcher or Silvia. There was only the two of them, together in one great, incredible uniting of the physical and the spiritual.

Afterward they lay, entwined, touching, yet separate, each relishing the wonder of what they'd been given. The candles had burned down and the moon was gone. There was only the two of them in the darkness. Silvia listened to the comforting steadiness of Fletcher's breathing. She stretched, reaching out to touch him.

Their hands met and fingers clasped.

He rolled over and propped himself on his elbow, loosening his fingers to caress her breast tenderly. "I suppose we can always come back, can't we?"

"Whenever we want," Silvia agreed.

"I love you, Silvia. I never thought that I could love someone so much."

"I love you, too, Fletcher. With you I feel strong and—I don't know how to explain it—invincible, perhaps. At least here, on the island. I don't know how strong I'll be when we have to return to Athens."

"And we have to go, don't we?"

"Yes. I think we do. This is a beautiful, wonderful dream, Fletcher, but that's all it is, for us."

"I know. I'd just like to take some of the dream back with us."

Silvia took Fletcher's hand and moved it lower. She spread his fingers across her stomach. "We are, darling."

"We are? I don't understand."

Then he felt her hands pressing him against her stomach.

"I'm pregnant, Fletcher. At least I think I am. Your native mid-wife says I am."

"Does that frighten you, Silvia darling?"

"No, yes, I guess it does. I never thought I'd

ever have another child. It will change everything for us, and I'd hate it if I get fat and ugly and you're sorry."

"Silvia, if you get fat and ugly, it will be because of me and I'll love every pound, just as long as you're all right." He frowned in the darkness. "You are all right, aren't you? I mean I thought women had morning sickness and got dizzy."

"Not so far. In fact I feel wonderful. Maybe it's because I'm so very, very happy. Maybe it's because you make me feel so very, very good." She slid his hand lower. "Maybe that's the answer, darling. So long as you keep making me feel good, I won't be sick."

"We'd better get back to the States, Silvia. I mean you'll need medical care, won't you?"

"The women on Hario Splendor have been having babies just fine without medical care," she argued.

"But they don't know anything else. We do. I'll start making plans."

"Not tonight, Fletcher. Not until after New Year's Day. I want to spend Christmas here, on this island with you."

"If you're sure."

"I'm sure. But I'm afraid I feel an attack of nausea coming on."

"Oh, my gosh. Maybe this was too much. Are you going to be sick?"

"Absolutely, unless you do something to stop it, like administering a little physical therapy."

She gave a little nudge, moving herself against his hand.

"Oh. Are you sure, Silvia?" He didn't need further encouragement. His finger dipped inside the moisture already collecting for him. His entry was rewarded with a movement that signaled Silvia's desire.

"I'm very sure, Fletcher. Love me, my Spider Man. Wrap me in your silver web."

There was ice on the ground when Silvia and Fletcher finally returned to Athens. The tall pine trees were bent to the ground in a silvery etching that looked more like a Christmas card than a late March afternoon. Fletcher and Silvia rented a car at the Atlanta airport and made the hour and a half drive to Silvia's home.

"Did Hallie say anything about our returning now instead of September as we'd planned?" Fletcher asked.

"Nope, just that she had a surprise."

"I suspect you have one for her, too."

"I expect so." Silvia didn't want Fletcher to know, but she was becoming self-conscious about her appearance. Though they'd taken time in Miami to shop for clothes that doubled as maternity wear, she still wasn't entirely comfortable with what was happening. On the island it had been natural and beautiful. Every pregnant woman shared her joy with everyone else.

Here, Silvia didn't know. When the car pulled into the driveway, Silvia caught his hand and squeezed it.

"Hang on, Mrs. Sims, I'm right here with you, willing to assume all the responsibility and the scorn."

"But Hallie will—"

"Hallie will know that we make love? That we've created a child? Of course she will, and so will Charlie, and Honey, and Greg. And if they don't, we'll call a press conference and announce it to the world. Oh, Silvia, I'm a happy man. And I want you to be happy, too."

Fletcher left the car and went around to open Silvia's door. He pulled her to her feet and into his arms, kissing her with all the passion they'd shared on the island. For a moment Silvia held back, then she felt herself responding, just as she always did.

The lights in Honey's house came on.

"Yoohoo, Silvia. Glad you're home." Honey's turban-covered head poked out her open window.

Fletcher pulled away and turned Silvia to face her neighbor. "Honey, guess what? We're having a baby! What do you think about that?"

"I think it may be the best thing that Silvia Fitzpatrick ever did."

"Not Fitzpatrick, Honey, Silvia Sims. We got married."

"Even better. Not as juicy for beauty parlor gossip, but good enough. Better get her inside before you two melt that ice and cause a flood. Night, folks."

"Fletcher, you didn't have to yell it out to the neighborhood," Silvia protested.

"Why not? The neighborhood gossip line will

spread the news faster than we can. Come on, darling, shall we go inside and share our news with our daughter and grandson?"

"Our daughter and grandson?" The words sounded so right. Silvia let Fletcher help her to the porch. Fletcher rang the bell anyway."

"The door is unlocked, Fletcher," Silvia pointed out.

"So was ours on the island, darling, but anybody knows better than to barge right in, even the natives."

Fletcher had been right. When Hallie answered the door, her face was flushed. She'd pulled on a robe, but even its fullness didn't conceal the rounded protrusion beneath.

Mother stared at daughter.

Daughter stared at mother.

Both began to laugh.

"I hope that means you and Fletcher are married, Mother. I'd hate to have to defend the very proper Silvia Fitzpatrick's already tarnished name to this community."

"Absolutely," Fletcher said, closing the door behind him.

"And I hope that means that you and Jeff have worked out your difficulties. I'd hate to know that Fletcher has to raise two babies."

"Well, let's just say we're working on it," the tall man said from the top of the steps. "Good to know you, Fletcher," Jeff said, shaking Fletcher's hand, and holding out his arms to Silvia. "Hello, Mom, welcome home."

A rush of feet at the top of the stairs announced

Charlie's arrival. "Fwesh! Gran! Mommy and Daddy are making a baby." He came to an abrupt stop, stared at his grandmother and began to smile.

"Gran making a baby, too?"

"Yes I am, Charlie. Is that all right with you?"

He studied the situation for a long minute before he smiled. "Yeah, if they aren't girls. Daddy and Fwesh and me need some ball players. My daddy's a coach, you know, for the Bulldogs. I'm going to play for the Bulldogs, too, just like my daddy when I grow up."

"And all ball players need to get their sleep, Charlie. Let's get you back to bed," Jeff lifted his son and started back up the stairs. "Are you coming, Hallie?"

"Absolutely, as soon as Mother and—my new stepfather get settled in."

"Go on, darling," Silvia said with a smile of pride. "Fletch and I will take the guest room, until we can find a place of our own."

"But, Mother, this is your house. You've always lived here."

"I know. But Fletch and I will need a new place. I'd like you and Jeff to have this house. I don't live here anymore."

Later, in the guest bedroom, Silvia squirmed, trying to get comfortable in the soft bed. She was more used to the mats they slept on in their island hut.

Fletcher sighed. "You're right, darling, this won't work. We don't live here any more. We can't make babies in this place. We can't even comfort the one you're carrying. I feel as if I'm smothering."

Silvia slid out of bed. She tiptoed to the hall and opened the linen closet. In a few minutes she returned.

"What are you doing?" Fletcher whispered.

"Making up our bed. Come and help me."

Silvia spread the comforters on the floor. Fletcher pulled the pillows from the bed and the covers. He put his arms around her and drew her down beside him. This time when he moved over her the bed didn't squeak, the floor didn't creak and Silvia didn't hesitate to respond.

When little Charlie bounded down the stairs the next morning to report that he'd waked his grandmother and Fletch, he was bursting with excitement.

"Mommy, Mommy! Gran and Fwesh fell off the bed and sleep on da floor. And—and—" he stuttered in the excitement of telling what he'd seen.

"Charlie, you didn't go into Gran's room, did you?"

"Fwesh say Charlie could come," he protested.

"And Gran, did she say you could come in?"

Charlie looked chagrined for a moment, then brightened. "Gran say the Night—the Nightwing put naughty words in Fwesh's mouth." He giggled. "She's going to wash it out with soap."

Hallie turned the bacon she was frying without looking up. "Nightwing? Are you sure about that?"

"That's a bird," Charlie said proudly. "Mommy, Charlie have blanket like Gran?"

Hallie looked up and gasped. "Charlie, where are your clothes?"

"Charlie take them off. Charlie want to sleep on floor and not wear clothes like Fwesh and Gran."

There was a sound of a masculine laugh and the slamming of the back door. "I think that's a great idea, son."

"Jeff, don't encourage the boy. It's bad enough that he's being told fairy tales."

"Why not?" He ruffled his son's hair. "But sleeping on the floor without clothes might be a bit cold right now, sport. Maybe someday when you're all grown up, you'll have a very wise woman to love you and keep you warm."

Jeff dropped the newspaper on the table, planted a loving kiss on Hallie's cheek and slid his arms around her, pulling her against him as he cradled her stomach with his hands. He whispered, "I think your mother and Fletcher have the right idea, Hallie. Want to try it?"

Hallie returned her husband's loving gaze with one of her own. She didn't understand what her son was saying about Nightwings and naughty words, but her mother set a very fine example, one that Hallie had always followed without question.

Upstairs in the bedroom, little Charlie's intrusion had already been forgotten, as Fletch pulled Silvia back into his arms. Below, in the kitchen, it didn't take long for Charlie to decide that March *was* too cold for nudity if he was going to take his father's suggestion that he go over and visit Honey. He quickly put his clothes back on and charged out the door to share his future sleeping plans with the neighbor he'd come to love.

As for the Fitzpatrick women, they had other ways to warm their bodies and fulfill their destinies. And without the least bit of shame, they were wickedly relentless in their pursuit of both.

When a heavily laden branch of ice broke from the tree beside Silvia's window, it grazed the side of the house, clattering as it fell. Silvia and Fletcher heard it. Hallie and Jeff heard it. But it was Honey who made the observation that it sounded like an explosion on the roof.

"No, Honey," Charlie insisted with all the assurance of a child. "It's a bird, a Nightwing bird. Gran says he makes Fwesh do naughty things."

"Is that right?" Honey asked, remembering the first time she'd seen Fletcher Sims, standing on Silvia's porch, wearing feathers and little else. "I always did like a wild night bird. Wonder what kind of food they eat?"

Across the crystal blue waters on the island of Hario Splendor, Moki and Luiani threw orchids into the lagoon and watched them as they rode the crest of the waves out to sea. The ceremony was an ancient one of welcome and farewell. It reached out to those who had gone away, calling them to the island. It had brought Fletcher back and with him had come the woman he loved. They would return again.

Moki and Luiani stood at the water's edge and smiled at each other shyly. They entwined their fingers and walked back into the trees.

For it had always been that way, those joined by love became part of the legend, part of the cycle of life forever renewed by the spirits of those who had gone on before and those who were yet to come.

SHARE THE FUN...
SHARE YOUR NEW-FOUND TREASURE!!

You don't want to let your new books out of your sight? That's okay. Your friends can get their own. Order below.

No. 21 THAT JAMES BOY by Lois Faye Dyer
Jesse believes in love at first sight. Now he has to convince Sarah of this.

No. 22 NEVER LET GO by Laura Phillips
Ryan has a big dilemma and Kelly is the answer to *all* his prayers.

No. 23 A PERFECT MATCH by Susan Combs
Ross can keep Emily safe but can he save himself from Emily?

No. 24 REMEMBER MY LOVE by Pamela Macaluso
Will Max ever remember the special love he and Deanna shared?

No. 25 LOVE WITH INTEREST by Darcy Rice
Stephanie & Elliot find $47,000,000 *plus* interest—true love!

No. 26 NEVER A BRIDE by Leanne Banks
The last thing Cassie wanted was a relationship. Joshua had other ideas.

No. 27 GOLDILOCKS by Judy Christenberry
David and Susan join forces and get tangled in their own web.

No. 28 SEASON OF THE HEART by Ann Hammond
Can Lane and Maggie's newfound feelings stand the test of time?

No. 29 FOSTER LOVE by Janis Reams Hudson
Morgan comes home to claim his children but Sarah claims his heart.

No. 30 REMEMBER THE NIGHT by Sally Falcon
Joanna throws caution to the wind. Is Nathan fantasy or reality?

No. 31 WINGS OF LOVE by Linda Windsor
Mac & Kelly soar to heights of ecstasy. Will they have a smooth landing?

No. 32 SWEET LAND OF LIBERTY by Ellen Kelly
Brock has a secret and Liberty's freedom could be in serious jeopardy!

No. 33 A TOUCH OF LOVE by Patricia Hagan
Kelly seeks peace and quiet and finds paradise in Mike's arms.

No. 34 NO EASY TASK by Chloe Summers
Hunter is wary when Doone delivers a package that will change his life.

No. 35 DIAMOND ON ICE by Lacey Dancer
Diana could melt even the coldest of hearts. Jason hasn't a chance.

No. 36 DADDY'S GIRL by Janice Kaiser
Slade wants more than Andrea is willing to give. Who wins?

No. 37 ROSES by Caitlin Randall
It's an inside job & K.C. helps Brett find more than the thief!

No. 38 HEARTS COLLIDE by Ann Patrick
Matthew finds big trouble and it's spelled P-a-u-l-a.

No. 39 QUINN'S INHERITANCE by Judi Lind
Gabe and Quinn share an inheritance and find an even greater fortune.

No. 40 CATCH A RISING STAR by Laura Phillips
Justin is seeking fame; Beth shows him an even greater reward.

No. 41 SPIDER'S WEB by Allie Jordan
Silvia's life was quiet and organized until Fletcher arrived on her front doorstep. Will life ever be the same again?

No. 42 TRUE COLORS by Dixie DuBois
Julian has the power to crush Nikki's world with the bat of an eye. But can he help her save herself? Can he save himself from Nikki?

No. 43 DUET by Patricia Collinge
On stage, Adam and Marina fit together like two pieces of a puzzle. Love just might be the glue that keeps them together off stage, as well.

No. 44 DEADLY COINCIDENCE by Denise Richards
J.D.'s instincts tell him he can't be wrong about his beautiful Laurie; her heart says to trust him. If they're wrong, it could be deadly!

Kismet Romances
Dept. 591, P. O. Box 41820, Philadelphia, PA 19101-9828

Please send the books I've indicated below. Check or money order only—no cash, stamps or C.O.D.s (PA residents, add 6% sales tax). I am enclosing $2.75 plus 75¢ handling fee for *each* book ordered.

Total Amount Enclosed: $_____.

___ No. 21	___ No. 27	___ No. 33	___ No. 39
___ No. 22	___ No. 28	___ No. 34	___ No. 40
___ No. 23	___ No. 29	___ No. 35	___ No. 41
___ No. 24	___ No. 30	___ No. 36	___ No. 42
___ No. 25	___ No. 31	___ No. 37	___ No. 43
___ No. 26	___ No. 32	___ No. 38	___ No. 44

Please Print:
Name _____
Address _____ Apt. No. _____
City/State _____ Zip _____

Allow four to six weeks for delivery. Quantities limited.